I CAN DO IT this time, her mind whispered. *This time, I can kill him. I can do it, because it's my job. I can do it to protect my world. I don't need Cal's permission—*

"You have it!" Cal shouted from behind me. "You have my permission, Lightbringer! Just do it! Do it fast!"

Relief suffused me.

My legs glided faster.

I raised the swords, ready to use both of them, one after the other, to cut him apart, to slice him to pieces.

I raised the first weapon, watching the Red Dragon's lips tilt up in a smile, just visible behind that smoke-like, misty swirl of light—

—then there was a flash.

He was gone.

Not partway, that time.

He disappeared entirely.

I brought the swords down anyway, one after the other, so fast the floating blades sliced down nearly simultaneously…

…but they cut through clouds of light, smoke and illusion.

They never once touched solid flesh and bone.

The light winked out.

Darkness stood where the Traveler king had been.

There was a loud *CLUNK* of metal where it slammed into stone.

The intensity of the blows jarred my arms.

I leapt back, more in instinct than thought.

When I looked down at the polished black rock—

—the pale, green-blue collar lay there, still flickering with that otherworldly light.

The Red Dragon was gone.

He was just… gone.

DARK GODS

LIGHT & SHADOW: BOOK 3

JC ANDRIJESKI

Dark Gods (Light & Shadow: Book Three)

Copyright 2021 by JC Andrijeski

Published by White Sun Press

First Edition

ISBN: 9798479963483

Cover Art & Design by Claire Holt of Luminescence Covers (2021)

Link with me at: https://jcandrijeski.com

Or at: https://www.facebook.com/groups/thelightsanctuary

Mailing List: https://bit.ly/JCA-mail

White Sun Press

For more information

about any book published by White Sun Press, please go to www.whitesunpress.com

Printed in the United States of America 2021

For my parents, Carol and Vince

THEY ARE NOT ALL THE SAME

*T*he silence in that underground cave, apart from that cold, humorless laughter of the old Traveler King, felt like death.

She should have known something was coming.

She should have known it wasn't over.

She should have known the danger had only started.

There wouldn't be any rest.

But Alexis didn't know those things, not at first.

Alexis had forgotten.

Somehow, she had forgotten what the Red Dragon was.

She had forgotten what it meant.

Here. In her world.

In her dimension.

She'd been so hell-bent on getting back to her post, back to the version of Earth she called her home, the place she was reasonably sure she'd been born. She'd wanted back here so badly, she'd completely forgotten all the calculations she would normally have made to execute a jump of that kind, with numerous non-Lightbringers in tow.

She'd forgotten about the price.

She'd forgotten the changes that would occur once they arrived.

She'd forgotten about the *price.*

Consequences.

There were always consequences.

Every inter-dimensional jump had them.

Worse, she'd forgotten the very nature of Travelers themselves.

All of it had overwhelmed her circuitry somehow.

The price of a jump. The fact that different beings had different magics and even different physiological characteristics on different worlds. The fact that she'd just cut herself and everyone else on her team off from the Ancients... that she'd severed herself from the source of her magical powers, and depleted herself of all of her remaining magic to do it.

After days... weeks... even months where she'd been imprisoned and held captive on that Traveler world, Alexis had grown accustomed to how Travelers existed in *that* dimension. She'd grown accustomed to how much more physical they were there, how much more substantial. How human-like they were.

On the Traveler world, it was easy to think of Travelers like any other species.

They seemed normal there.

Magicked, yes, but relatively normal.

There, on their home world, Travelers seemed like vampires, or seers, or fae, or elves... or even Lightbringers themselves.

They seemed far less mysterious there.

Frankly, they *were* far less mysterious there.

Alexis had forgotten that Travelers didn't manifest that way here, in her world.

Here, Travelers weren't physically solid.

When meeting Travelers here, Alexis had questioned

whether they were made of bones, skin, and flesh at all. She'd questioned that of Cal. She'd questioned it of every Traveler she came across on her own version of Earth.

She'd forgotten.

Being on the Traveler world, she'd forgotten all of that.

She'd allowed herself to normalize Travelers, mostly from spending so much time with them on their own world. She'd begun to see them just like any other people. She noted their odd customs, the bits of their history Cal fed her, but her mind gradually categorized them as a new species of supernatural with which she'd gradually grown more comfortable.

Over that time... weeks and months of that time... she told herself they were an odd, strange race. At the same time, her mind ceased to view them that way.

On their own world, Travelers were as physically solid as a tree. They were... human-like. It wasn't a perfect comparison, but on their own world, it felt close.

But on Alexis' version of Earth, Travelers didn't exist that way at all.

Alexis had forgotten.

Somehow, she'd forgotten all of it.

She'd forgotten the cost of portal jumps, the differences in magicks and manifestations. She'd forgotten how strange Cal seemed to her, the first time they'd met. She'd forgotten the way he *appeared* to her, like a shadowy apparition on the catwalk overlooking her club's main floor. She'd forgotten the flickering changes of his outline.

She'd forgotten how otherworldly he'd seemed.

She'd forgotten the abilities he'd wielded to confuse her, to sneak up on her, to evade whatever security she had in place around the portals.

She'd forgotten how alien he'd been, how entirely super-natural, as his matter seemed to arrange and re-arrange itself, right in front of her eyes, even while they were having sex.

He'd seemed so… insubstantial to her back then.

So utterly ephemeral.

More like some kind of nature spirit than a real person.

It caused her to trust the Traveler King less than she might have otherwise.

How had she forgotten all of that?

Well, maybe *forgot* wasn't the right word.

It simply hadn't been her priority.

The fact that here, on *her* version of Earth, Travelers turned into shape-shifting, inexplicable, multi-dimensional, spirit-creatures, tricksters who hid their true nature and even their physicality, simply hadn't been at the top of her list of things for Alexis to think about over the past few days.

It certainly hadn't been on her mind while they were actively running away from The Others and their minions.

Anyway, it wasn't usually something she *had* to think about.

Usually, she hopped dimensions alone, and even then, infrequently.

But alone.

Alexis was a Lightbringer.

She didn't change.

Lightbringers didn't change, regardless of which dimension in which they found themselves. They remained the same. Constant. A single composition, a single set of characteristics, a single type of existence.

Lightbringers were made to hop portals.

Lightbringers did not change.

Travelers did.

"What in the hell?" Devin's voice held an open shock.

Fear lived there, but his words came out as a bare murmur.

Jules let out a shriek.

Warrick, the big bodyguard for Cal back on his home world, the one whose race Alexis hadn't yet pinpointed, stepped back from the Red Dragon in alarm.

"What in the foul realms is this?" Warrick spat the words, his voice a cold demand. "What is happening to them? Explain this, Lightbringer! *Explain it!*"

Alexis didn't.

Alexis couldn't... not really.

She looked at Cal, the only Traveler she'd ever really known well enough to consider asking about such things, but there was no time to ask. Any questions she had about the nature of a Traveler on her world could only come too late.

It was too late.

Feeling the reality of this... really *feeling* it... Alexis turned back to stare at the Red Dragon with all the rest of them.

She stared at him in the dark cave under Penang Hill.

It was already too late.

She reached back, with both of her hands. Gripping the handles, she unsheathed her swords, but even though she moved quickly, seamlessly, faster than any human or vampire, she knew it was too late.

Everything seemed to happen in slow motion.

A death-like silence fell over her, over Devin, over Warrick, over Cal and the other Traveler guards... over Jules. That silence subsumed everything, expanding through the high walls of the underground cavern as she stared at Cal's father, the Red Dragon.

She could feel it.

She could feel it, and she remembered.

She remembered her first impressions of Cal.

She remembered him standing on the catwalk of the Red

Whip, a tall, ephemeral, mist-like apparition, as if he only existed halfway in this realm.

She listened to the Red Dragon laugh, heard the sheer triumph in the sound.

Then she watched as his skin, his hair, his entire outline grew insubstantial, as if made of smoke and light more than flesh and bone. His hands morphed. His legs began to scatter as if made of dust.

The skin of his face morphed the most.

Those changes also appeared the most dramatic. His skin turned to lit clouds. The smoke and clouds turned his eyes to stars, spread down his jaw and to his neck...

...his neck.

Where the collar professed to hold him.

The Red Dragon's eyes changed from dark blue to a violent, bloody scarlet.

The silence in the cave, apart from that cold, humorless laughter, really did feel like death... like all of them waited to die, waited for the Red Dragon to kill them.

Gripping the swords in both hands, she looked back at Cal.

She moved towards the Red Dragon, but her eyes remained on his son.

She saw his skin turn to smoke and lit fire, too.

She saw it among the Travelers, all of them, as their bodies adjusted to this world.

But it was different this time.

Maybe because she'd shut the door.

Maybe because she'd shut *all the doors.*

Or maybe because the Travelers hadn't yet found their equilibrium here.

Time slowed to a crawl, to an excruciating set of slow-moving increments.

Alexis heard the others continue to react around her—her

childhood friends, Devin, the alpha werewolf, Jules, a half-fae training to be an Earth Witch, Warrick, the... whatever the hell Warrick was... the Travelers meant to hold on to the Red Dragon as guards.

Alexis heard some of them shouting.

Alexis heard some of them scream.

A part of her watched in the periphery of her vision as they all watched the Red Dragon.

Alexis wielded her swords out in front of her.

She never stopped crossing the black-rock floor.

She aimed her feet, her eyes, her focus on the ex-king of the Traveler worlds.

I can do it this time, her mind whispered. *This time, I can kill him. I can do it, because it's my job. I can do it to protect my world. I don't need Cal's permission—*

"You have it!" Cal shouted from behind me. "You have my permission, Lightbringer! Just do it! Do it fast!"

Relief suffused me.

My legs glided faster.

I raised the swords, ready to use both of them, one after the other, to cut him apart, to slice him to pieces.

I raised the first weapon, watching the Red Dragon's lips tilt up in a smile, just visible behind that smoke-like, misty swirl of light—

—then there was a flash.

He was gone.

Not partway, that time.

He disappeared entirely.

I brought the swords down anyway, one after the other, so fast the floating blades sliced down nearly simultaneously...

...but they cut through clouds of light, smoke and illusion.

They never once touched solid flesh and bone.

The light winked out.

Darkness stood where the Traveler king had been.

There was a loud *CLUNK* of metal where it slammed into stone.

The intensity of the blows jarred my arms.

I leapt back, more in instinct than thought.

When I looked down at the polished black rock—

—the pale, green-blue collar lay there, still flickering with that otherworldly light.

The Red Dragon was gone.

He was just… gone.

2

AFTERMATH

"Well, Jesus, Mary, and Joseph... *Now* what?" Devin demanded.

He stood there, panting.

He was still using the remnants of his clothes to wipe the blood off his arms and chest.

Alexis didn't know why he bothered, honestly... at least half of their group was covered all or partway in splatters of blood. Alexis herself had vampire blood drying on her clothes, skin, hair, and face. She even had it stuck in her fingernails, and the creases of her elbows.

Wiping themselves off with ripped up clothes definitely wasn't going to cut it.

They'd need to find a discreet place to wash off before they got around normal people once more, or they'd end up in a Malaysian jail cell, booked for murder while they scoured the mountaintop for dead bodies.

Really, they should try to deal with it before they left the cave at all, much less returned to the hiking trails that led up and down the mountain. They couldn't do anything about the Red Dragon or anything else from a Southeast Asian prison.

Alexis remembered the underground lake.

Of course.

Crap on a popsicle stick... her mind must really be screwed up, for her to have forgotten that was down here. Hell, that deep, still lake filled most of the damned cave.

Re-sheathing her swords with a ringing sound, she looked around at everyone, feeling her jaw harden, feeling all of their eyes on her.

She could only glimpse white faces, illuminated by the fae light Jules made, that still hovered a few yards overhead, illuminating most of the cave near the portal.

"We must open the door!" Cal growled.

He glared at Devin, then looked back at me.

"Now, Lightbringer! Right now!" Pausing, he glared around at all of them. "My father will be attempting the same... even as we speak!"

Alexis scowled.

His words felt true.

She opened her mouth, about to answer him, when a female voice shouted.

"Donree!"

One of the Travelers, a small, blue-haired female, ran back in the direction of the portal, not far from where the Red Dragon vanished.

Alexis blinked, watching as the female knelt down on the stone, next to a male who sprawled on his back, his hand over his throat.

Shit. She'd forgotten.

One of them had come through injured.

She'd more or less assumed he was already dead.

Glancing at Cal, she saw the grim look he gave her in

return, and realized he'd thought the same. She began walking over to where the big male had fallen.

Cal, Devin, and Jules followed her.

"Is he alive?" Alexis asked when she got close enough.

She didn't mean to be callous, but the female Traveler glared up at her.

"I don't know," she shot back. "Perhaps you'd like to run him through with one of your swords, Lightbringer… in case he might slow us down?"

Alexis felt her jaw harden.

"No," she said, subduing her voice. "Can you help him?"

The female Traveler bit her lip, shaking her head.

Alexis got more of an *I don't know* out of that head-shake than a straight *no.*

She looked at Cal. "I don't know Traveler magic," she said, matter-of-fact. "Or Traveler physiology. Can any of you heal him?"

Cal looked at her, his expression grim.

He glanced at Jules.

"Do you have a healer's magic, fae-ling?" he said.

Unlike before, he didn't say the last part like it was an insult.

Jules frowned, bit her lip, then reluctantly shook her head.

"Could we bring him to a human hospital?" Alexis asked.

"Weren't you thinking just now that would land us in jail?" Cal said, frowning.

"If it saves his life—"

But Alexis' words were cut off.

The male Traveler was choking, gasping, convulsing as he tried to breathe.

The female Traveler held the cut on his throat, tears in her eyes.

"Donree," she said to him. "Brother, hold on. Hold on. We

can bring you somewhere. We can fix you. You cannot give up…"

Alexis heard it in her voice that time, though.

The Traveler was dying.

She felt a pain in her chest when she remembered all of these Travelers were likely friends, that they'd likely worked together, served together for years. Not only that, they'd lost a number of their people already, to the silvery snakes in that cave on the other side of the portal.

Borghen approached the male on the other side, kneeling down across from the female on the stone.

The male slowly stopped convulsing.

Borghen held his hand, even as he looked over the rest of his body for wounds.

He opened the armored vest he wore, and a huge gash was there, like a baseball had punched its way through his side.

Jules gasped.

Devin grimaced, taking a half-step back. "Fuck. That looks bad."

The male Traveler moved less and less.

The rest of them stood there, watching.

Alexis stood there, too, feeling utterly helpless.

She could see it on Borghen's face, even more than she could hear it in the female Traveler's voice. The male was dying. It was too late to stop it.

As she thought it, Cal took her hand.

When she looked at him, he nodded, his face grim.

Then both of them looked down at the body of the downed Traveler, and watched their friends stay with him until, a few minutes later…

Donee, a Traveler Alexis had never known, drew his last breath.

3

DEATH AND MACHINES

"Well, that's just great," Devin growled, sitting down on one of the Sphinx's forelegs, rubbing his face with a muscular hand. "The portals are closed. We've lost that Red Dragon fuck. We've got no idea where he is. And now one of us is dead."

"He'd died before he got here," Cal cut in.

Cal's voice shifted, growing overtly warning.

"That didn't happen here. You saw the gash in his side. And he *wasn't* the first. We lost two others, before the rest of us made it through—"

"And?" Devin looked up, glaring at the Traveler King from where he sat. "What's your fucking point, *Cal?*"

"My point is, at least *we're* still alive. We all could have died in that cave. All of us. Several of us *did* die—"

"You think I don't know that?" the werewolf growled. "*You* were the one just bitching and screaming at 'Lex for closing the gate!"

"Perhaps I was wrong—" Cal began, angry.

Devin cut him off with a heavy laugh.

"*Perhaps? Perhaps* you were wrong?"

"Shut up." Alexis shot warning looks at both of them, her voice colder than either of theirs. "Stop this bickering. Now."

She aimed her stare at Cal.

"Can you track him? Your father? We need to find him, Cal. Right away."

There was a silence.

In it, they all watched the Traveler King as his eyes slid out of focus.

None of them moved or spoke for a few seconds.

Then Cal exhaled an exasperated breath, shaking his head.

"No." Cal frowned, his eyes still distant. "I can't."

"But you did before—" Alexis began.

"Yes," Cal broke in. He met her gaze. "I did track him before. I can't now. I've been trying. Even before this, I tried. As soon as he disappeared, I tried."

He looked around at all of them, his expression grim.

His eyes returned to Alexis'.

"He's blocking me... somehow. The only thing I can think, is he likely has help here already. Loyalists. People he seeded in this dimension, beyond the guards he left at the portal itself... meaning the ones wolf-boy already disposed of."

Devin growled, probably at being called "wolf-boy."

Cal scarcely looked at him.

"From what I can see," he said, still speaking seriously to Alexis. "My father had help as soon as he got free of the cave. Maybe they were waiting for him out there. Maybe he called them and they came. Or maybe they were guarding the cave itself. Whatever the truth of it, that's where it changed... as soon as he reached the surface. That's where his presence disappeared."

At Alexis' pursed mouth, Cal exhaled, shaking his head.

"That's where I lost him, at least. It's possible he felt me and blocked me out on his own... but I've never known him capable of that before. I tracked him through the cave itself. I watched him exit out the opening into the sunlight, and then he just..."

He made a *poof* gesture with his fingers.

"...I can't explain it. I've never tried to track him in this dimension, so it's possible I can't follow him over as long of distances here. Whatever the cause, we'll have to find him another way. On the plus side, maybe he can't track us, either."

Alexis frowned. She definitely wasn't going to count on that.

Not after last time.

"You're right of course," Cal said, obviously hearing her. "We can't trust it."

He slid his fingers through his hair.

Exhaling, he subdued his voice, looking up at her.

"What about you?" he said, motioning towards the tattoos on her arms. "Can you teleport us? We need to re-open the primary portal. I imagine it will have moved, yes? So we cannot do it from here. You'll have to take us to the new location."

Alexis frowned.

Before she could answer him, Jules spoke up. The half-fae sounded unnerved, angry, afraid... possibly even full-blown freaked out.

"So, explain to me why we would *want* to open that damned door again, when we barely got out of there with our lives?" Jules looked between them, biting the inside of her cheek. Her eyes landed on Alexis when they paused.

"Wouldn't we *not* want to do that?" she pressed. "Wouldn't opening that portal be the *last* thing we want to do?"

She looked between them again, biting her lip.

When Alexis didn't answer her, Jules took a deep breath,

as if trying to calm herself down. Walking backwards, she sat down on the stone arm of the Sphinx, a few feet away from where Devin sat and across from Cal.

"If that Red Dragon asshole…" She glanced at Cal, wincing, as if remembering the asshole was Cal's father. "Look, no offense, but if that *psycho* is going to try and re-open the doors, shouldn't we *avoid* doing that? For as long as possible?"

"Damn good bloody question," Devin muttered.

"No, it's *not* a good question," Cal muttered back.

The Traveler King's gaze grew cold. He shifted his stare between Jules and Devin.

"We need to open the portal. That my father wants to do it only makes that need more urgent. It's a matter of life and death… of the fate of not just your world, but of all of them. Don't you see?"

"No," Devin growled. "I don't see. *Why* would we want to do that?"

Cal's pale gold eyes shifted to the werewolf.

"Because we must," he said. "Trust me, wolf… I don't think you want *my father* to be in control of the portals to this world." Cal looked at Jules, and his voice grew even colder. "Assuming he can do it in the first place… even *with* help… which he likely can't. He'll just make a hell of a mess trying. Knowing him, he'll blow up the damned *world* trying. That, or he'll attempt to enslave Alexis again and make *her* do it for him."

"What?" Jules folded her arms, the fae light hovering over her head. "He can't do that." She looked up at Alexis. "Can he?"

Devin growled at Cal.

"Why would he care so much?" he said.

At Cal's derisive laugh, Devin cut him off.

"And seriously? 'Blow up the world'? Sounds a bit melodramatic, O Mighty White Dragon. What the hell does that even mean? How would he go about blowing up an entire planet, exactly? He doesn't really have that kind of power, does he?"

Cal gave Devin another scathing look.

"Only a few beings on this world are actually *powerful* enough to reopen the doors, wolf. Most of those containing that much power can... and have... sent entire dimensions back to the Stone Ages at one time or another."

Clenching his jaw, he added in a darker mutter,

"...Easily half of those beings are of the Dark, not the Light. My father would not solicit help from beings of Light. As he would say, 'too many strings attached, Caliginous. You must always find the *practical* beings. You must always work with those who can be bought off, or who have the same goals as yourself...'"

Cal's voice sounded bitter by the end.

He aimed that darker stare at the rest of them.

"Make no mistake. Anyone my father looks to for help will be an ally of The Others already. He will go to the Dark Arts, and he will try to get his way and damned be the consequences for anyone else... even if it kills half of your planet."

Cal turned his stare back to Alexis.

"More and more, I think he is likely to have agents of his here already... regardless of whether anyone met him outside the cave. There are likely powerful agents of The Others on your world... more since he forced me to kidnap you, and make you my wife."

Still scowling, he added, "There might even be beings already in this dimension who can open the gates for him. Or begin ripping apart the world until *you* agree to do it."

Alexis felt her jaw harden.

She was only half-listening to Cal, though.

Now, she jerked her head in the direction of the opening to the box canyon.

"Come on," she said. "We cannot stay here. We need to wash up."

"No!" Cal snapped. "Are you not hearing me, Lightbringer? He will destroy *your* world first. He will destroy it, and he will enslave *you*... and within months, years at most, all of the worlds will be in darkness because of us."

Alexis didn't blink.

"We need to wash up," she repeated.

"No!" Cal snapped. *"Gods of Darkness and Light!* You must take us to the new portal, Alexis! We cannot delay! We *cannot*. Do you really think I would lie to you on something so essential? If my father can, he will open a portal, but not to the Ancients. He will open it only to the world of The Others. He will conquer this world with their armies... and then he will move to the next. And the next. And the next after that. Each time, only opening each world's portals long enough to let his invading armies through."

Cal motioned towards where the portal door had been, at the base of the great Sphinx.

When he did, his coat, arm, and fingers rippled with that light-infused smoke. Compared to how his father had looked before he disappeared, the light glowed faintly, more like a reflection on mist, but Alexis couldn't help but follow it with her eyes.

"Open it!" he demanded. "Please, Lightbringer! For all of our sakes, you must *try* at least. You are our only prayer of stopping him!"

Looking away from where she'd been watching the smoke and light and cloud-like ripples coil around his arms and legs, she met his gaze.

"I can't," she said frankly.

"What?" His pupils dilated visibly. "Why not?"

"My magic is entirely depleted. I can't feel it at all." She motioned towards her tattoos, which were inert, flat in color. "There is nothing to summon. Closing the gates drained me down to the core... I had to draw off the rest of you to even complete the spell."

There was a silence.

After a few seconds of watching them all stare at her, Alexis sighed.

"You are right, Cal," she said next, her voice subdued. "The primary portal is no longer here. It moved. Assuming it isn't gone entirely... and that its erasure wasn't the end point of that spell I did... I will take us there as soon as my magic comes back."

"*Will* it come back, 'Lex?" Jules's voice vibrated with worry.

Alexis looked at her.

Thinking about her question, she shrugged.

"I don't know," she said honestly.

The silence deepened.

"How long would it take?" Jules asked next. "If it was to come back? How much time would it take for your magic to fully regenerate?"

Alexis thought about that question, too.

In the end, she could only shrug a second time.

"I don't know."

"What the fuck does that mean?" Devin muttered.

Alexis looked at him.

She looked at Cal next, who was staring at her, a half-shocked, defeated look on his face. Feeling all of their stares on her, she felt her jaw harden.

"I didn't do it on purpose," she said. "I was trying to save us."

Cal closed his slightly-ajar mouth with a snap, and averted his gaze.

"Gods of the Deep." The Traveler King combed a hand through his hair. "Where is it? Can you feel where the new portal is moved to, at least?"

"No." Alexis exhaled in frustration. "No, I can't. I can't feel anything at all."

There was another silence.

That time, Cal wasn't the only one who felt and looked defeated.

Alexis exhaled, fighting her own frustration.

"Can we just go wash off?" she said after another beat. "I need to think before we do anything rash, and none of us can go around human beings here, not looking like this. The clothes will draw enough attention, much less—"

"Wait," Devin cut in. "You really can't feel the portal anymore?" His voice sounded close to angry now. "Could your magic really be *gone*, 'Lex? For good, I mean? No portals, no Lightbringer... that kind of thing?"

He seemed to be thinking even as he spoke.

He swallowed as his own words hit him, right before he met her gaze.

"Could you just be a regular human now, Lex? With unusual tattoos and some cool martial arts skills?"

Alexis looked at him, pursing her lips.

Then, in lieu of answering, she threw up her hands.

"I don't know," she said.

"Well, that's just great!" Devin snapped. "Are you *kidding me*, 'Lex? How the hell are we supposed to—"

"SHUT UP!" Warrick shouted. "EVERYONE SHUT UP! SHE SAID SHE DOESN'T KNOW SO SHE DOESN'T KNOW!"

They all stared at him.

The big male scowled, aiming his gun up at the high cavern's ceiling.

He pulled the trigger.

He pulled it again.

Presumably, Warrick intended for the noise of the gun going off, multiple times, inside a cave, to get all of their attention, maybe to snap them out of their dogpile on Alexis. Maybe he wanted them to get out of there, away from the dead bodies on the cave floor, away from the smell of the dead and the pitch black cavern.

Whatever he intended, the weapon's firing mechanism didn't cooperate.

Instead of letting out a blast of purple and blue living fire, the gun's mechanics emitted a loud, ominous *CLICK*.

Frowning, Warrick tried to fire the gun two more times.

That time, the branch-like weapon sparked, letting off a puff of greenish smoke.

To Alexis, it looked like someone poured water on an electrical outlet.

The smoke grew thicker.

Warrick cursed.

He started shaking the gun. At first, it looked like he was trying to get it to start up again, like he thought shaking it might fix the problem.

Then, cursing louder, he released the firing mechanism, shaking his whole arm, the same arm around which the bulk of the gun coiled.

Alexis might have found it funny under other circumstances.

But then Warrick yelped in real pain.

Alexis saw the gun start to change color, turning from a darker gray-green to a lighter, more vibrant orange.

Warrick was shaking his arm violently now, clearly trying to get the weapon off his arm. He managed to get most of it off his wrist and forearm, then pried the rest off his bicep and the left side of his waist and ribs. He threw the whole thing to the floor and it smoked and sparked, even as it grew lighter in color.

"It's hot," Warrick muttered. "It's damned hot."

He looked at the others, holding out his arm in warning.

"Don't get any closer... and mind your own weapons!"

Alexis had already taken a wary step backwards.

Now she took another.

Jules, obviously thinking along the same lines as Alexis, got up from her seat on the Sphinx's arm and took a few steps back of her own, walking towards the mouth of the small box canyon. Devin got up and followed her.

"Is it going to explode?" Jules muttered, glancing at Alexis.

Borghen and the other two Travelers were backing off now, too.

At the same time, they started trying to take off their own guns.

Alexis frowned, looking at Warrick, then Cal.

"Well?" she said. "Is anyone going to answer her question?"

Cal scowled. "How in the gods would I know if it will explode? I have no idea what your dimension does to our weapons. Do you think I have ever brought a weapon of this kind to your world before? Do you think I would ever risk such a thing?"

Alexis opened her mouth, closed it.

She really didn't have a good answer.

Of course, any being who came through the portal armed would be considered an immediate threat. They would be disarmed... by force, if necessary.

Likely by Alexis herself.

Cal must know that.

All beings who traveled the portals knew the rules.

If they didn't, they didn't last long.

The Traveler King grunted, folding his arms.

"Of *course* I know that," he muttered. "Gods of the Other-worlds, wife... after all this, you still think me and my people to be idiots. You seem to think everyone *not* from this solitary, isolated, backwards dimension to be feeble-minded in some way..."

Alexis fought a smile for some reason.

It might even have been nerves.

It may have just been tension from nearly dying, the dead bodies, the death.

Either way, it was difficult not to laugh.

She considered making a crack, then glanced down at the strange, branch-like weapon on the stone, wondering if they needed to make a run for it.

The weapon had ceased to grow brighter, though.

In fact, now it seemed to slowly be growing darker once more.

Alexis watched it cautiously as it turned from that bright orange back to a duller gray.

She stared at it until she was reassured it wasn't likely to explode.

Then she looked around at the other Travelers.

She noted they all now held their weapons gripped in their hands, having removed them from where they'd wrapped around their forearms and biceps. Clearly, they didn't want to experience whatever just happened to Warrick.

"Leave the rest of those guns here," she told them. "Blunt weapons, knives, anything without moving or chemical parts... you can take those with you. I'm assuming they should be safe. Drop anything you don't need or want, and we'll go."

The remaining three Traveler soldiers hesitated, looking at one another.

Then Borghen seemed to agree with her.

He released the gun he held, letting it clatter to the cave floor.

Then, using his other hand and arm, he began unwinding what might have been a second weapon from around his ribs and waist. The way he did it, the strange piece of equipment looked like a heavy and muscular snake, one he had to coax to let go of him.

The other Traveler soldiers, of which only two living ones remained, followed his lead.

Warrick scowled, but pulled a second weapon off his own belt.

He left it on the Sphinx's arm, along with an armband and a small, gray, stone-like device. He took an earpiece out of his ear and left that on the cave floor, then dropped another device as well, similar to the one Borghen had unwrapped from around his waist.

Alexis watched them gradually disarm, one alien machine at a time.

Once they'd finished, she motioned in the direction of the lake that lived past that opening.

"I was serious about the lake," she said. "We all need to bathe before we go up. Those of us covered in blood will need to wash off everything. Hair. Hands. Faces. Necks. Clothing. We can't do anything about drying off. And if we can't get the blood off our clothes, we'll need to figure out a way to get rid of those, too, even if that means sharing the articles of clothing we have left. Meaning the ones that aren't bloody."

She watched them look at one another.

None of them grumbled aloud, but from the looks on their faces, they wanted to.

"We stay together." Alexis' voice grew into a command. "We wash off. We do what we can with clothes... then we make our way down the hill to the city below. Together.

Whatever compromises we have to make on clothing we can remedy once we get to the airport. I'll call my people and have funds transferred. We should be able to buy whatever we need."

Seeing the blank stares greeting her inside the fae light, Alexis sighed internally.

Lugging this many off-world supernaturals around with her wasn't going to be easy.

In fact, it was going to be a bona fide pain in the ass.

She didn't see that she had much choice, though.

Now that they were back on her turf, Alexis was unquestionably in charge.

4

LEAVING THE CAVE

*A*bout the only *good* thing that came of the disorientation afflicting all the creatures in Alexis' newly acquired, mostly non-human, oddly-dressed entourage was…

They all followed her instructions.

After that initial freak-out in the cave, they all took her orders and instructions without so much as a grumble of protest, and followed them.

All of them did.

Including Cal.

Including Devin.

For the most part, unless she counted the occasional cold, blatantly-accusatory glare from Warrick (which she didn't), Alexis got basically no pushback at all from anyone in the motley crew that stumbled through the portal with her.

Of course, Alexis couldn't really take credit for the quiet obedience of the others.

The deaths had clearly shocked them, the Travelers especially.

The Traveler guard with the cut throat had clearly been a

friend, someone they cared about. Alexis knew they might also be reacting to the deaths of the other two Traveler soldiers as well, the ones they lost inside the pyramid to those worm-creatures of The Others.

Cal, Borghen, and the other two Travelers talked briefly about maybe burying the Traveler with the cut throat, or maybe carrying him to the lake, setting him on fire, or covering his body in stones.

Alexis hadn't weighed in on that discussion.

In her view, that was between the Travelers.

She stood there with the rest of them anyway, watching the corpse's eyes grow glassy, then milky, right before his skin began to change, in a way no dead human's skin did so soon after the last breath. Black veins grew visible under increasingly translucent skin, and Alexis watched, horrified and fascinated, as the dead Traveler's eyes sank deeper into his skull, even as the lips dried and the blood at his cut throat grew black, turning hard as glass.

Eventually, the female Traveler who had knelt there stood up.

Shock shone clearly in her eyes, but she didn't say a word.

Alexis had already gathered that she'd known the dead one well, seemingly better than the rest of them. She had perhaps even known him intimately.

Whatever the nature of their relationship, the others were gentle with her.

None of them spoke about the dead man directly, other than what to do with his body, but Alexis saw Borghen rubbing her shoulders, and stroking her hair. Alexis saw Cal do the same, and the other male, who Alexis didn't know, held her hand.

Eventually they decided to leave the male's body behind.

They all followed Alexis to the dark lake, and there, all of them washed off the blood—or as much of it as they could in the darkness and the cold.

They couldn't see well enough to assess the blood on their clothes, so they decided to do that when they returned to the surface.

Alexis led them out of the cave, retracing her and Cal's steps from when she'd come down here the first time, what felt like years ago now.

When they hit the Earth sunlight, Alexis felt like an alien from another world.

The familiarity and oddness of being back home nearly made her dizzy.

The sky, the trees... even the dirt itself... felt shockingly, painfully familiar.

Only then did it hit her to wonder what the price would be, for bringing Devin and Jules through. Presumably, there'd been some price on Cal's world, for taking them there. Hopefully, whatever it was, it simply got reversed when they came back.

The Travelers shouldn't have brought a price with them.

It was the peculiarity of Travelers that they could hop portals without paying a price.

Alexis herself, as a Lightbringer, shouldn't cause any imbalances, either.

Warrick, whose race Alexis still couldn't be sure of, may have a price or may not.

Regardless of prices and consequences and the lack thereof, there was still an element of feeling out of step from this dimension, after being away for so long.

Alexis wondered if it was what Devin had said.

Was she just human now?

Was her Lightbringer status revoked, now that there were no portals to protect?

Would she be allowed to have an ordinary life?

The thought was strangely, almost painfully alluring.

Of course, from what Cal had said, she wouldn't be allowed to live a peaceful, ordinary life for long. If she really was just a human now, that meant the Red Dragon would likely take over their world unopposed, and she would die an ordinary death, or be enslaved with the rest of the ordinary humans.

Still, for a brief, shining breath, she could almost imagine it.

Being ordinary.

Having a life free of the burdens she'd had placed on her since she was a child.

Even as a fantasy, it felt lovely.

Like a beautiful dream.

As for those feelings of unreality, Alexis swore she saw the same disorientation and relieved, bewildered, off-kilter looks on Devin and Jules when she looked at them. It struck Alexis as almost funny that the three persons who appeared the most off-balance in their group were the three who actually *belonged* here...

...The three who called this dimension their home.

Devin and Jules both looked at her with that understanding in their eyes.

Still, no one spoke.

Devin and Jules didn't speak.

The Travelers didn't speak.

Warrick, whatever he was, didn't speak, either.

Alexis didn't push any of them to break the silence.

With a motion of her head and arm, she led them down the mountain instead, skipping the mountainside train to bring them down on foot.

As they walked, they discarded some clothes, trading layers and pieces with one another until they were more or less covered with things without noticeable traces of blood.

"It's just until we get to the airport," Alexis reminded them.

They all nodded, but none of them spoke.

Alexis couldn't even be sure they comprehended what she'd said.

Their silence and compliance gave her time to think, at least.

It gave her at least a *tiny* amount of mental space to decide what happened next.

The basics came to her more or less naturally.

Get them to the airport.

Get access to her money.

Buy them clothes.

Feed them... and possibly caffeinate all of them.

After that, things got a bit more variable.

When they reached the bottom of the hill and managed to hitch a ride into Georgetown, and then grab a bus to the airport. While on the bus, Alexis finally broke the silence long enough to ask Cal, Borghen, Jules, Devin, the other Travelers and Warrick, what they thought should happen next, after they took care of basics.

Her instincts told her to get them out of Penang.

She told them she suspected the Red Dragon was probably still here, but that she still wanted to travel somewhere else, somewhere where she had connections, preferably a city housing one of her clubs, although not necessarily the one in Los Angeles.

Alexis confessed to all of them, she could likely do nothing for them here.

She could likely do nothing for them *anywhere* without supernatural and real-world help, given she had no access to her magic at the moment, and not so much as a smart phone.

If *they* could also do nothing—meaning, if the Travelers

themselves had no way to track the Red Dragon, or to fight him once they found him—Alexis suggested they all leave.

Regroup.

Go somewhere where Alexis had access to her resources.

Go somewhere with access to magics, to spells, to someone who could use them.

Track the Red Dragon.

Then go after him.

Even if the Red Dragon was still here, which Cal and the others agreed with her was likely to be true… temporarily, at least… Alexis had no way to find him.

Cal had no way to find him.

Alexis knew no one in this part of Malaysia.

She saw no point in flying south to Kuala Lumpur either, since she didn't own a club in Kuala Lumpur.

She had a club in Singapore, but it was new, and she knew few people there, either.

Besides, from everything Cal had said, they likely had to worry about the Red Dragon hunting *them,* as much as they had to worry about finding him. In the short term, it was likely Cal's father was looking for a way out himself, assuming he hadn't left already.

The portal had moved.

There was no reason for any of them to stay without it, and with the Red Dragon now loose on her version of Earth, Alexis felt drawn to be somewhere more familiar. She wanted access to friends, help, employees, spell-books, her magical objects, her bank accounts, a decent hotel… not to mention the local supernatural talent.

That meant putting all of her new "friends" on a plane— or possibly a ship—either back to Los Angeles, or, what was likely more practical, to Bangkok first, since that was a heck of a lot closer to where the Red Dragon likely was, and Alexis was well-connected there.

They could spend a few nights in Bangkok, utilize the club and connections Alexis had there, track the Red Dragon using the local magical talent, and then, once they'd located him, either go straight to him to neutralize him… or, if they found someone in Bangkok who could do it, try to open the portals back up themselves.

If they couldn't find the Red Dragon from Bangkok, Alexis would take them either to London or straight to L.A., depending on what made the most sense.

In the end, while a large part of Alexis wanted to go straight home, she decided Bangkok made the most sense.

Realizing she'd massively over-explained *all of this* to the seven people now traveling with her, she fell silent, looking around at all of their faces for reaction.

She saw very little.

In the end, though, Cal nodded.

"Okay," is all he said.

It didn't occur to her until later that they'd likely only heard one out of every three words she'd said. Between losing their friends, the portal jump, the Red Dragon's disappearance, the hike down the mountain, and whatever else, they all looked utterly exhausted.

For the same reason, she didn't press them again, or try to get a clearer answer.

She receded back into her own thoughts, instead.

Bouncing in the back of a rusted-out, ancient Mercedes truck, one that didn't feel like it had any shock absorbers left at all, she stared sightlessly out the window at the jungle and falling rain, watching the scenery go by as they made their way towards the small international airport on the island of Penang.

All of them were soaking wet and covered in mud.

Then again, even before it started raining, they'd all been wet.

Half of them were wet from the lake.

The other half were soon wet from the humid air as they pressed through the jungle to reach the city below.

Then it started to rain.

Being Asia during the monsoon season, it wasn't the light, sprinkling rains one normally got in Los Angeles. This was one of those Southeast Asian downpours that wet you to the skin in seconds, the kind for which umbrellas were practically useless.

Her entire group looked like drowned rats.

They looked miserable.

She felt for them.

Strangely, she felt for all of them… a lot.

Perhaps it was because she was back on her own world.

Somehow, she'd become *responsible* again.

She'd become accountable to those under her protection.

Even without her Lightbringer magic, she'd become the person in charge.

Now, looking around at all of them, she felt guilty, knowing she'd soon have to make them uncomfortable again.

But it couldn't be helped, and she told herself they'd be a lot happier once she got them into a nice hotel, with room service and jacuzzi bathtubs and views of the *Chao Praya* river at night. A little alcohol might not be amiss, either, given everything.

Maybe a lot of alcohol for some of them.

In the meantime, they'd all just have to power through.

5

BEING HUMAN

*P*utting them on the plane was probably the most nerve-wracking.

Jules, with the help of Cal and Borghen, had to use magic to get them through immigration, and even though it worked without a hitch, it made Alexis damned nervous.

It might have been partly because she wasn't the one doing the magics—which, if she was being honest with herself, *always* made her slightly nervous, since she was a control freak through and through—but she swore that wasn't all of it.

She felt eyes on them.

Alexis swore she felt eyes on them the whole time they were there, but she could never find anyone watching them, or pin down the feeling well enough to share it with the others.

Immigration was nerve-wracking for more ordinary, human reasons, too.

If they'd been caught, they likely all would have spent at least one night in jail.

Not to mention, Alexis didn't generally *use* magic for that kind of thing.

She didn't abuse her abilities to mess with the human authorities.

She didn't flagrantly break human law.

But in this case, they had little choice.

There was no way to do what they needed to do legally.

There was no *fast* way to do it without magic.

Even if they crossed the border to Thailand on foot, they would be forced to do so illegally. If they crossed via a train or bus... same thing, it would be illegal.

Even to get them fake passport would take days.

Alexis knew that.

She knew her reactions were illogical.

Still, it felt like too much exposure—for the Travelers, especially—to buckle them into seats on a commercial airline, first class or no.

Again, she could think of no better alternative.

Her own magic, which really had been entirely depleted in that last, cataclysmic, End-of-Days spell, didn't seem to be coming back in a hurry.

After the hour or so walk it took to get down the mountain of Penang... and the other half-hour she spent talking to people at the Bangkok Club and arranging for tickets and cash and hotel reservations in Bangkok, and a car to be waiting for them at the airport... and the time it took to take the bus to the airport on Penang (even the bus fare ended up being paid by her club)... and the time in the airport buying and changing into new clothes, grabbing coffees, egg sandwiches, dried mangos, chocolates, figs, and other snacks for the plane... even after all that, Alexis *still* didn't feel so much as a flicker of her Lightbringer magic returning.

She felt like a battery drained of juice.

She felt like a computer console that had shorted out.

The one time she took a few minutes to try and perform a

pale test of her power, at the airport gate while they waited to board, Alexis felt nothing.

She saw nothing.

Nothing at all happened.

Her tattoos remained inert; they didn't glow. They didn't even flicker.

She felt nothing between her hands. None of the usual geometries she summoned for portal gates appeared from her fingers.

Her magic was gone.

It really was *gone,* possibly even permanently, like Devin said.

For now, at least, she was functionally human.

She had no idea for how long.

It shouldn't have surprised her, really.

That last spell to close the primary gate drained every last ounce of her reserves. Just to perform it, she'd had to draw from every living thing around her. Given she'd never done a spell like that before—she'd never done one even *remotely* like that—she had no idea when she'd be replenished again.

If ever.

It might not be ever.

Alexis hadn't really thought about that possibility until Devin said it, but now it made a kind of sense to her.

She might not get her powers back until the portals re-opened.

She might not get them back even then.

In the meantime, they had to be content with the more human, less-fantastical forms of transportation. Alexis' resources, while still considerable, were now primarily of the human variety. Apart from whatever help she could get from other supernaturals—both those currently traveling with her and whoever she could get in touch with once they reached Bangkok—she was magic-free for now.

"It will come back," Cal muttered.

He adjusted his back in the seat next to hers, frowning.

When she glanced over, he turned his head as well, giving her a dark look.

His sculpted mouth hardened.

"It *will* come back," he repeated. "I promise it, Light-bringer."

Looking away from her, he added, lower,

"...It must. Therefore, it will."

Alexis didn't bother trying to pull apart *that* logic.

Instead she sighed, sinking deeper into the airplane seat next to the one occupied by the Traveler King. Across the aisle from her, also in First Class, Jules and Devin sat together.

The row in front of them held Borghen and one of his two remaining Traveler guards, the male. Alexis thought she'd heard the others calling him Montu.

In front of her and Cal sat Warrick and the other remaining Traveler guard from Borghen's team, the female.

Alexis had discovered she was named Vulca.

Now Vulca, who had been covered in even more blood than Cal had been, after trying to save Donree, wore all new human clothes, in the style of *this* dimension.

Her skin and hair had been cleaned in the lake under the mountain, then again in a Malaysian airport bathroom, after Jules saw Vulca naked and insisted.

They'd been helping the Traveler figure out her new Earth clothes.

Jules washed Vulca's hair in the airport shower using actual shampoo, and blood still ran down the Traveler's body and into the drain. Even after the lake, she'd had blood in her ears, and under the clothes she'd worn, and under her fingernails.

Most of the clothes Vulca had worn before they helped

her change had been Borghen's. She'd left pretty much all of hers near the cave on Penang Hill.

Alexis herself bandaged up the few cuts she found on the Traveler's skin.

Most of the blood hadn't been hers.

Vulca's *physical* injuries had been minor.

Looking at the ghost-white skin of the Traveler soldier's face, the haunted look in her dark eyes, the near-palpable exhaustion etched in her features, Alexis strongly suspected the female Traveler was still in shock.

Not all that surprising, really, given that Vulca had seen at least three of her fellow Traveler-soldiers get murdered right in front of her.

After watching all of the Travelers struggle with things as simple as clothing and food at the airport, Alexis again considered keeping them in Penang a few days. She'd been worried they might all become unstable, and wanted to give the Travelers a little time to recover.

When she voiced the thought cautiously, Cal and even Vulca herself immediately vetoed her tentative offer.

Both had been adamant.

Both had been entirely inflexible on that point.

Both wanted to look for the Red Dragon.

They wanted to *hunt* the Red Dragon.

And really, Alexis was good with that.

She worried about the mental state of the Travelers still, but she comprehended the urge to combat trauma with action.

She comprehended it down to her very soul.

Given their desires and Alexis' own urges, they could not stay.

So she had her people book them on the first flight to Bangkok.

6

AN OLD RACE

"*I* think I could die of happiness right now," Jules said, her words muffled as she lay face-down on the enormous, king-sized bed. "I really could," she mumbled. "I could die."

She lay there a few seconds longer, then sighed.

"Maybe one of you should just drop something heavy on my head. Make sure you get me in one blow, though. I don't want to feel a thing."

Devin leaned down and smacked her on the ass, making her jump, and making Alexis snort in surprised laughter.

Giving the half-fae one of his devilish grins, Devin growled.

"No sleeping yet, munchkin," he announced in that growl, using a nickname that started for some reason in high school. "We have food to feed an army coming up here. And you said you'd try out the jacuzzi with me. I'm holding you to that."

Despite her brief amusement, coupled with a nearly over-whelming relief at hearing Devin sounding almost like himself again, Alexis couldn't manage to stay focused on her two best friends for long.

She'd just had a brand new phone brought to her by one of the employees of The White Rabbit, the club she owned north of Sathorn in Bangkok, not far from the *Chao Praya* river.

She had them program in the numbers of all the clubs, the names of all the managers, and any contacts they could pull off the cloud for her personal account.

They'd done her one better.

They'd found and downloaded a clone of her entire phone.

Now she had them working on doing the same for Jules.

Their actual hotel—which was both famous and infamous as a monument to colonialism—also held the dubious honor of being the most expensive place to stay in Bangkok. It sat right on the river, an old-school, colonial-style structure all in white, with columns and wooden shutters and fountains and a newer set of four outdoor, lagoon-style pools. The original structure had been built by the British, and maintained over the years in a nearly-pristine version of its former glory. They'd added on to that structure, added the pools, expanded the gardens, and bought up property on either side to build restaurants and shops.

Unlike most of the old buildings in this part of town, which had either been torn down, or allowed to slowly sink into dereliction, this one had historical value, if only for the dignitaries who had stayed there.

For the same reason, it had been renovated a few dozen times since it was originally built, all while retaining most of its colonial charms, the architectural ones, at least.

Alexis, Jules, and Devin currently occupied the largest suite the hotel offered.

She'd more or less rented out the entire top floor.

She would need to check in on the Travelers soon, make sure they had everything they needed, but first things first.

She dialed in a number from memory, and let it ring.

…and ring.

And ring.

It rang maybe thirty times.

Maybe forty.

Finally, there was a click.

A voice on the other end rose, even as the being completed the motion of raising the receiver to her mouth and ear.

"Alexis, my dear…" the low, accented voice purred. "You simply cannot take a hint, can you? You must have known I felt you calling."

"It's important—" Alexis began.

"Of course it is." The being sighed. "When is it not?"

"I need you. It's important, Mara. Not only to humans. Not only to Lightbringers."

Silence fell over the ancient landline.

"You did this?" the voice said next. "This thing with the doors?"

"Yes."

"You cut us off from the Ancients? From the Light?" The being's voice held a discernible tinge of anger now. "*You* did this? The one tasked with protecting our world? Do you have any idea of what you've done?"

Alexis bit her lip.

She glanced over at Jules and Devin.

Both of her high school friends now watched her from the enormous bed, Jules half-submerged between folds of the thick, white, duck-down duvet.

They stared at her avidly, eyes alert, their ears metaphorically pricked.

They clearly heard something in her voice—or, in Devin's

case, possibly he heard the words of the female seer through the phone's receiver.

That damned werewolf hearing was unreal.

"I did do it. I did know what it would mean… more or less." Alexis said, tearing her eyes off her friends. She focused back on the seer on the other end of the line. "I apologize. It was necessary. I am trying to fix it now. That is why I need your help."

The being scoffed openly at that.

"Necessary. This is always what the Dark Ones say. Right before they burn your world to the ground. They say *it is necessary.* This isn't even the first time I've heard such a thing today, Alexis Poole—"

"Mara," Alexis cut in, warning. "I don't have time for this. If you want to verbally chastise me over the decision I made, you'll have to do it in person. Preferably over a decent tea, something in the oolong family."

Falling silent, she practically felt the other being turning over her words, hearing the various unsaid meanings living around them.

With an effort, Alexis subdued her voice when she next spoke.

"I really can't do this over the phone," she said. "I would like to do it person. I can't spend the time it would take to explain everything to you like this."

"What does that mean?" the seer said warily.

"It means I'm in Bangkok," Alexis answered, her voice a touch more warning. "Can we meet? There is still a grave danger. You know this. You just said as much. If you want me to make things right, I require your assistance."

Alexis practically heard the being frown.

"A grave danger? Here in Bangkok?"

Thinking about the question, Alexis frowned.

"Perhaps. I'm less clear on that end of things. In fact, that's part of what I'd hoped you might help me with. But I cannot speak of it on the phone," Alexis repeated, her voice a touch warning. "We should really speak in person, Mara."

"You will come here?" The seer sounded doubtful.

"I could. Or you could come here. That would possibly be more comfortable. For both of us."

Alexis bit her tongue, staring out the window of the Elephant Colonial Gardens Hotel.

She looked out over the river, fighting another wave of exhaustion.

"I'm at the Gardens," she added, using the local name for the hotel.

The seer still didn't break the silence.

"The Elephant Colonial Gardens," Alexis clarified.

That time, she practically heard the seer roll her eyes.

"Yes, dearest. I understand this. I have only lived in Bangkok for about three hundred years now. I only watched this monument to ego, avarice, decadence, and hubris being built by your beloved humans—"

"You'll come?"

There was another silence.

Then the being exhaled, clicking its tongue in that odd manner of seers.

Alexis had learned the clicking contained a world of nuanced meanings, normally derived from context mixed with how hard, soft, subtle, or whatever nuanced combination of clicks the clicking seer employed with their tongue. This one struck her as a kind of sigh mixed with impatience, possibly mixed with a denser annoyance.

Seers were an odd race.

An old race.

"No," the seer said next. "You will come to me. Old Town. The same place. In three hours."

"Three hours? Why so long?"

"Three hours. It is that, or we do not meet, Lightbringer."

"But why?"

"I do not explain my schedule to you, either, Alexis Poole."

Alexis bit her lip, glancing at the clock.

She considered offering her club instead.

In the end, she realized she needed the other being too much to argue details.

Still, she kept the impatience out of her voice with an effort.

"I will be there," she said only.

7

A STRANGE PULL

"Who the *hell* was that?" Devin said, incredulous.

Before she could answer, he shook his head, his muscular hands planted on either side of him on the mattress. He looked at Jules, then back at her, his expression half bemused, half wary.

"You really do know the damnedest people, 'Lex."

Alexis refrained from muttering that most of them weren't people.

She considered trying to explain Mara in some way, or the even stranger seers she'd met over the years, but before she could decide whether or not it was worth the time and brainpower it would take to find words, given the timeline they were on, the doorbell buzzed for the penthouse suite.

Without a word, she turned on her heel.

She walked directly to the door, opening it without preamble.

When she saw the row of waiters standing there in white jackets and white suit pants, paired with black ties and black shoes, Alexis stood aside so they could wheel in their rolling carts overloaded with plates of food.

She smiled a little bemusedly as cart after cart went by, thinking to herself it was always dangerous when you put a werewolf in charge of ordering the food.

Within minutes, the waiters had all six carts set up as a kind of buffet line, halfway between the large table in the middle of the common area of the suite, and the even larger flat-screen television set under a horseshoe of sectional couch pieces.

After Alexis signed everything, leaving them a generous tip, they bowed, and walked out, smiling as they wished everyone an enjoyable meal.

Alexis only then wandered over to look at the uncovered plates.

Plates, bowls, platters, with a large hot-pot of white rice in the center of the rolling cart they placed on one end.

They even had a cart devoted entirely to drinks—both the alcoholic and the non-alcoholic varieties, including coffee, tea, milk, espresso, juice.

Sniffing the Thai spices and eyeing the various Thai dishes, mixed in with tandooris, curries, seafood dishes from various regions, noodle dishes, sushi rolls, and appetizers, she felt her tummy growl. There was a plate of grilled squid, another of *Pad Thai*, three kinds of fried chicken, tofu green curry, *Pad See Ew*, *Tom Yum* Soup, Pineapple Fried Rice, Thai steak salad, red and yellow Thai curries with seafood, along with an assortment of colorful cakes, meat skewers, different-colored sauces, mango slices, papaya salad, cucumber salad, fried shrimp, fresh summer rolls, fried spring rolls, chicken satay, lamb meatballs…

It was a *lot* of food.

It was a *hell of a lot* of food.

Alexis found it exhausting even trying to catalogue it all.

In the end, she scooped up a plate and a bowl and began filling them up.

She more or less picked things at random until the plate was full, then she stopped.

She set her plate and bowl down on the low coffee table in front of the couch, and sat down cross-legged in front of it.

Devin walked in and burst out in a laugh.

"Don't mind us, 'Lex," he smirked, glancing at Jules with a laugh before he looked back at Alexis sitting on the floor. "Go on. Eat without us."

"You have noses," Alexis retorted, picking up one of the meat skewers she'd grabbed and dipping it in peanut sauce. She grunted, looking over the skewer at Devin. "I know you have a nose. You'll just have to follow it when you're hungry, wolf-man."

Devin shook his head, but the smile never left his face.

He walked to the same side of the row of room service carts as where she'd started, scooped up a plate, and proceeded to load his plate even higher than hers, mostly with the meatiest items he could find.

Jules protested a few times as she lagged a few platters behind him, seemingly positive Devin would eat all of the good stuff, particular all of the good stuff from one of the dishes she especially wanted to eat.

In the end, though, Jules had about a third as much food on her plate as Alexis did, and maybe a fifth as much as Devin.

All three of them sat around the coffee table on cushions.

For a few minutes they didn't even talk.

As if by mutual agreement, they just scooped up their eating utensil of choice—fork, spoon, ladle, knife, fingers— and proceeded to eat.

After he'd demolished maybe half of his plate, Devin finally looked up at Alexis.

From his facial expression, the food was working its magic on him already.

Devin looked calmer.

He also looked more focused, like he was back in strategy-thinking mode.

More annoyingly, he also wore a bit of a smirk.

"Where's the husband, 'Lex?" He took a big bite of a fresh summer role, dipped in sweet chili sauce. He grinned at her, but she saw a harder scrutiny in his eyes. "I thought you'd be sharing a bed with him. Not with us."

Alexis sighed a little internally.

The truth was, she felt a pull to go check on Cal, and possibly the rest of his Traveler friends, and even Warrick.

She'd once more explained the food thing to him, reminded of their last adventure with take-out in Los Angeles, and explained the phone to him.

Borghen, Vulca, and Warrick listened while she spoke, but they'd all seemed as baffled and borderline annoyed and uninterested as Cal himself.

The other Traveler, Montu, had been in the shower, and making semi-pornographic noises from his enthusiasm over the hard sprays of hot water.

Alexis had done her best to ignore that.

Truthfully, she'd been focused on Cal, even then.

She'd felt Cal disapproving of her announced sleeping arrangements, and wanting to speak to her alone.

She'd ignored that, too.

She felt Cal even now, somewhere in the background of her mind.

She could almost see him there, muttering curses under his breath in his Traveler's language, pacing the length of their suite, which was set up more like a large, two-story apartment or townhouse, complete with a high-ceilinged living room, a separate kitchen, two bathrooms, and three bedrooms.

This suite, the one Alexis had claimed for herself, Devin, and Jules, was smaller, with only two bedrooms, one and a half bathrooms, and smaller kitchens and living rooms.

She could feel Cal fuming about that, too.

She could also feel his paranoid certainty that she would be sharing one of the beds, not with him... and not with Jules.

Alexis thought he was being an ass.

She thought his bizarre jealousy over Devin was juvenile.

Far more annoying, however, was the fact Alexis couldn't say for certain she disagreed with him entirely, either.

Not about Devin, of course.

More about the sleeping arrangements.

She felt a pull to share a bed with him, too.

Frowning as she chewed on a piece of curried chicken, she didn't realize she'd never answered Devin until he cleared his throat pointedly.

She glanced up, and that time, the werewolf looked actually annoyed.

"He's not sleeping in here, is he?" Devin grumbled.

Alexis hesitated.

Before she'd decided how to answer, another voice rose by the door.

"He is," Cal said, his voice openly annoyed. "...If he has anything to say about the matter, he most decidedly *is* sleeping in here. And not alone, wolf. And certainly not with you."

Alexis turned, looking up at the Traveler King from where she sat, half-cross-legged on the floor. She had one knee propped up so she could use it as an armrest, and still gripped the wooden stick with curried chicken on it with one hand.

She looked up at Cal, who she remembered suddenly she'd felt compelled to give her extra hotel room card-key to.

She replayed in her mind what he'd just said to Devin, and wanted to be annoyed.

She wanted to snap at him for glaring at Devin, even now. For looking almost...

...offended.

He looked offended with her, she realized.

She didn't think she was imagining that.

Obviously hearing her thoughts, the Traveler King grunted.

She looked at him, blinked, and realized she *wasn't* annoyed.

She wasn't annoyed with him at all.

Even after he'd yelled at her after she'd closed the portal gates, "annoyed" didn't come close to the emotion she felt as she looked at him.

Pulling herself gracefully to her feet, using only the muscles of her legs as she slid back up to her full height, she walked directly to him.

She walked like she hunted.

Slow, graceful, without a wasted movement or sound.

Her mind went totally blank.

That happened when she hunted, too.

She walked directly up to the Traveler King without a single falter in her step, without pausing even to get his permission. Without so much as a hesitation, she wrapped her arms around him, and snuggled up into his chest.

8

NOT ALONE

*I*f she'd surprised him, that surprise was short-lived.

His arms wrapped around her at once, pulling the length of her against him, and within seconds, she felt the Traveler King making a low, rumbling, purring sound in his chest.

She also heard Devin growl.

She felt Devin staring at her, too, incredulity wafting off him like a scent.

Jules might have stared at her as well, but she did it a lot more quietly.

Reluctantly, after what felt like too-short of a time, Alexis pulled out of her embrace with the Traveler King. Sighing a bit, she stepped back, folding her arms across her chest. When she looked up at Caliginous's face, she found him staring down at her, his irises a serene, pale blue.

He didn't smile, but she saw emotion there.

She saw emotion in his face, but most of all, in his eyes.

She saw enough emotion, she forced her own eyes away.

She found herself looking at Borghen instead.

"Did you order food?" she asked the big Traveler politely.

"As it turns out, we have far more than we could ever need. So if you *haven't* ordered yet, you're welcome to eat as much of ours as you want..."

Borghen blinked, then smiled.

Without being asked a second time, he walked over to the coffee table (*...and right up to Jules,* Alexis' eyes and mind couldn't help noticing...).

The big Traveler looked on the verge of sitting down, possibly to eat off of Devin's, Jules', and Alexis' plates, or some combination of the three, but Jules held up a hand. She wiped her mouth with a napkin, and stood up, moving far more gracefully than Alexis herself had.

"You move with the grace of a queen," Cal murmured, low enough that it seemed meant only for her. "She moves like a sweet child. You move like a warrior queen."

Alexis snorted a little.

Even so, she smiled at him.

She knew he meant it as a compliment.

She also knew how rare it was, that someone compared her to Jules and complimented her. Not that she begrudged her friend, but she did sometimes feel invisible beside her.

Cal snorted at that, right before he took hold of her hand.

"I think you are delusional, wife," he said quietly.

She shivered at his words.

She didn't look over, though. Instead, she watched Jules with Borghen, unable to help but be amused by the interactions of the small-boned half-fae and the Traveler with the massive shoulders and probably a foot and a half of height over her.

She found them weirdly adorable.

Taking the big Traveler's wrist, Jules tugged Borghen over to the row of room service carts. Reaching the end, she picked up a plate for him from the stack, and handed it to him without a word. Then she took him down the row of carts, pointing out the various dishes and trying to describe what they tasted like.

Alexis couldn't help noticing that Montu and Vulca listened carefully to Jules' descriptions, as well.

It struck her that Cal listened with interest, too.

Then she heard his stomach growl.

Bursting out in a startled laugh, she rubbed his stomach through the dark gray T-shirt he wore, a find from the gift shop in Penang's airport.

He quirked an eyebrow at her, and she grinned back at him.

"What the fuck, Alexi?" Devin muttered.

She gave her friend an irritated look that time.

Devin still sat cross-legged on the floor. Now his arms were crossed too, and he looked up at her, obvious annoyance in his expression, coupled with a glaring anger in his eyes. Most of the latter seemed aimed at Cal. The former seemed reserved for her.

"Are you really *dating* this guy?" Devin said. "You really are. This piece of shit kidnaps you, collars you... and now he's your *boyfriend?* How does that work, 'Lex? Care to enlighten me? Or Jules? Because she was wondering, too."

Alexis ignored the question.

She looked back at Cal.

"I told you how to order food," she reminded him, lifting an eyebrow.

He smiled, tilting his head to acknowledge her words.

"We found the process you outlined... complicated."

Alexis snorted another involuntary laugh.

"The room service menu proved to be too much for the Traveler set?" she teased.

"Perhaps."

He held up a hand, motioning in some facsimile of a

shrug. Smoke and light wisped around his outline, strangely fascinating to watch.

Equally strangely, it didn't disturb her.

She actually found it pulled at her in some way, making her want to touch him again, maybe even to play with the light and shadow that coiled around his skin.

She wondered why that was.

Stepping out of his arms for a second time, she remembered where she would need to be going in less than two hours, and felt her work mode fall back over her.

Almost like changing channels in her mind, possibly in her body as well, she felt herself click back into that more stripped-down version of herself.

Her mind cleared. Her posture straightened.

Even her voice changed, growing more precise, clipped.

"I have to go somewhere," she said. "Related to our problem."

Hearing the silence her words produced, she paused.

It wasn't only Cal who fell silent.

She looked around at the rest of them, noting the frown on Devin's face, the surprise on Jules' as she looked between Alexis and Cal. Jules seemed less annoyed with her than Devin, but Alexis found herself thinking the half-fae saw something between her and Cal.

Something perhaps she herself had missed.

Cal grunted. "Of course she has seen things," he muttered. "She's half-fae."

Alexis considered answering that.

She also considered asking what he meant.

In the end, she did neither.

There would be time for such questions and explanations later.

If it was anything serious, or dangerous, Jules would definitely pull her aside and tell her right away. At the moment, "dangerous"—or even "serious" per se—wasn't really the vibe she was getting off Jules.

Curious, maybe.

More than that, she got a flicker of understanding off her friend.

Something along the lines of... *Oh, okay. So that's what it is. I get it now.*

Alexis wasn't sure if that understanding was aimed at her behavior around Cal, Cal's behavior around her, or both of their behavior together, with one another.

"I *suspect* the last of those," Cal murmured, frowning faintly as he watched Jules. "But truthfully, I cannot be certain either. I *do* think she approves more now. Than she had, that is. She is not worried about you, about this, the way she was... whatever that wolf says."

Alexis looked back to the Traveler King.

"Most of them can stay here," she said. "For my errand. This shouldn't take more than a few hours."

Devin let out a low growl.

Alexis gave him a warning look.

Then, thinking about her own words, she folded her arms.

Still thinking, she took another step backwards, if only to give herself space to think. As she did, she did her best to ignore the increasingly intense stare she felt from Devin.

Not to mention the stare she felt from Cal.

"Really, *everyone* can stay," she added, glancing around at the rest of them. She included the other Travelers in her look that time. "Most of you definitely *should* stay. Sleep. Eat. Try to replenish your energy as much as you can. At the very least, sit in the hot tub for a while and maybe watch a movie. Get some rest."

She looked at Jules specifically.

"...But really try to sleep if you can. Go for a swim first, call people you need to call to let them know you're okay. Do whatever will help you recharge for a few hours. There's a good chance we might need to leave Bangkok soon, so the more you can rest up here, the better."

Seeing Devin frown in a different way that time, she raised a hand, preempting the protest rising to his eyes.

"This isn't a dangerous contact," she informed him. "More a strange one. And one easily spooked, so I can really only take one of you with me. Normally, I would go alone. Mara is likely to be twitchy enough as it is."

Thinking about that, she hesitated.

Then she made up her mind.

She looked at Cal.

When she spoke next, she aimed her voice solely at him.

"...But I thought you might want to come with me."

"What?" Devin growled. "Him? *He's* the one you think should go with you on this weird errand you won't tell us anything about? No." He shook his head. "No. Absolutely not. You're not taking *him,* 'Lex. No way. If you can only take one person, take me. Or Jules."

Devin glared openly at the Traveler King.

"...Someone you can trust. Someone you can *actually* trust, 'Lex."

Alexis glanced at him.

She didn't respond to his anger that time, either.

She looked back at Cal, instead.

She gauged the expression on his face.

"It's about finding him," she added. "Your father. If it wasn't, I would likely just go alone. I could *still* go alone. If you'd rather sleep, that's no problem at all. But I wanted to offer it. I wanted you to come with me, if you'd rather hear from her yourself."

Devin growled, low in his chest.

Jules, who'd been in the process of sitting down cross-legged beside him, after leading Borghen through every step of the improvised buffet, smacked the werewolf in the chest.

Devin jumped, startled.

Then he went silent.

He glared at Jules, but stayed silent.

Alexis could still feel Devin seething, but her own focus remained on the Traveler King.

Cal's expression didn't move.

His form flickered in and out around the edges, but the changes were still small; he remained more or less in one shape, one solid outline.

It struck Alexis as strange suddenly, that she wanted Cal to come with her.

She wasn't in any way asking to be polite—she really *did* want him to come.

She could have just as easily have gone alone.

In the past, it would have been far more within her comfort zone to go alone.

Liking or not-liking a person wouldn't have factored into it.

She would have made some excuse to appease Devin, to leave him behind. Or, depending on her mood, she might simply have announced an executive decision to go alone.

Back home, in Los Angeles, where she wasn't surrounded by her friends or sharing a hotel suite with them, she wouldn't have given it a second thought. Unless she had a specific, tactical reason to include them, like asking Devin's pack to track, patrol, or hunt a specific person or group of entities, she wouldn't have told anyone anything.

She just would have left.

She could have done that here, too, come to think of it.

She could have simply eaten and walked out the suite door.

But now that she was back on her home turf, and had the

opportunity to *finally* do things the way she'd always done them, she found herself asking the Traveler King to come with her.

After months of being tied to Cal in his world, then being surrounded by his guards—or at least the one bodyguard, Warrick—Alexis was back on her home turf.

Here, on this world, she was accustomed to doing things alone.

She was accustomed to doing just about everything alone.

Cal cleared his throat.

Alexis lifted an eyebrow.

"Can I eat first?" he said.

His eyes, which had been a light amber-color, slowly began morphing to a pale green. They transitioned seamlessly to an even paler violet. He glanced over his shoulder at where Borghen continued to heap different-colored spoonfuls of curry and stir fry on his plate.

"That smells quite... odd. But I find I'm very hungry suddenly."

Alexis nodded, keeping her own expression still.

It only struck her a few seconds later that some part of her wanted to laugh.

9

WHAT I AM

"I've called in with the pack," Devin muttered, hanging around outside the walk-in closet while she got dressed. "You probably heard some of that. I called Gabriela, too."

Alexis nodded, not bothering to comment on what she'd heard.

"Good," she said.

"I've only really let them know I'm okay so far," he added. "But I'm going to call Vic back. I was going to tell them more about what we're doing now, and where we are. Do you want any of them to come here? To Bangkok?"

"Wait on that," she said. "We may be going to them soon... we'd only cross over and under one another on the Pacific."

"Right," Devin muttered.

From his voice, which reached her from just outside the walk-in closet, he'd only half-heard her as he thought through their options.

She could also tell he was a little disappointed.

Talking to his pack, if Alexis knew him at all, probably

both relaxed him slightly and made him anxious as hell. He would want to go to them, and soon.

She couldn't exactly blame him.

Alexis had just taken a shower.

Cal had gone back to his room, presumably to do the same.

Jules and Devin were more or less monopolizing the phones while they dealt with the people in their lives who'd more or less thought they were dead or kidnapped for the past week.

Apparently the minions of The Others had left Devin's house trashed enough to completely freak out his pack, not to mention Jules' adopted family, Devin's girlfriend, and all of Jules' and Devin's friends and neighbors, not to mention everyone who worked at the Red Whip.

Thinking about that, Alexis sighed.

There might be more fallout from this whole mess than she'd fully realized.

They would need to come up with some kind of semi-plausible cover story, and soon.

Jules' family, in particular, would have been losing their minds.

They also knew absolutely nothing about magic or Jules' half-human status. They simply adored their quirky, adorable, and strangely intuitive daughter with the odd friends.

Alexis sighed again.

Once she'd finished with her shower, she'd left the bathroom wearing the hotel's complimentary fluffy robe. Which was a good thing, since she'd found Devin on her bed, using her new mobile phone, which was plugged into the wall by the king-sized bed—presumably because Jules was using the phone in the other room.

Devin had left it plugged in while he spoke to whoever it was he'd called.

When he mimed an apology with his hands and eyes, Alexis waved him off.

She grabbed the bag of new clothes she'd bought in Penang and entered the walk-in closet to dress. Before she did that, she started hanging up clothes for later, only to have Devin hang up his call and begin talking to her through the closet's open door.

She didn't mind.

Devin was family.

Plus, she knew him well enough to know he'd be pacing out there, thinking out loud, muttering under his breath... not trying to glimpse her naked ass in mirrors or in surreptitious peeks through the partly-open door.

For the same reason, she answered his muttered musings when it seemed appropriate, even as she was throwing on brand-new, clean, civilian clothes. She thought about his words now as she tore the tag off the soft, gray T-shirt she'd picked out of the pile.

Tossing the piece of paper in a small wastepaper basket on the floor, she frowned, thinking along with him.

"When you talk to them next, tell them to check the gate," she said, her voice distracted. "And ask them about those smoke creatures. Find out if they've been seeing them around town or in Griffith Park while we were gone."

Still thinking, she added,

"And have one of them call up the other packs. Have them check with the locals about the London gate, the one in Moscow, and—"

"Yeah, yeah." Devin had gone back to pacing. "I'll have them check all of them."

"What about Gabriela?" Alexis asked next.

"I asked her to keep an eye on us," Devin said. "I could tell she wanted to anyway. She said she'd put magic tracker-type things on all of us, make sure no one got too close. She thinks she knows what to look for, after what she sensed at the Old Zoo portal."

Alexis nodded, frowning faintly.

She'd almost forgotten Gabriela had been there that night.

Now she tried to decide if there was some way she could use it.

"Have her look at my magicks, too," Alexis said after a beat. "See if she can figure out if the problem is permanent or temporary... and when it might come back, if it is temporary. It'd be nice to know if there's been any change. We won't have to rush onto a plane if I'm able to use a portal to get us all back to Los Angeles."

There was a brief silence.

Then Devin exhaled.

"I already did ask her to do that," the werewolf admitted. "When she said that thing about knowing what The Others look like... magically, that is... I asked her to look for Charles, too. And any beings, really, with that kind of energy. She was going to get with her coven and call me back. She said they're all aware something is 'different' anyway. When I told her about you having to close the portals, she was pretty disturbed. I guess they were having an emergency coven meeting about it today anyway... well, today, their time. Early in the morning in Los Angeles..."

Alexis nodded, buckling up the belt she'd looped around the new pants she'd bought.

"Is your house all right?" she asked next.

There was another silence.

"I forgot to ask," Devin admitted.

"Ask them."

"Next time," Devin said, dismissive. "I'm not worried

about my house, 'Lex. Vic would've had Ray and Hannah fixing the glass doors and windows and changing the locks that very day…"

Ray and Hannah were two pack members who owned a company as construction contractors. Remembering that, Alexis nodded.

"Of course," she murmured.

"Anyway, I didn't tell *any* of them much yet," Devin added, combing a hand through his dark hair. "Right now I'm still coping with the 'we thought you were dead!' thing. It's kind of taking center stage over whether or not someone trashed my house while I was gone."

"I get that," she said patiently. "But those smoke creatures know where you live. We need to know if they've been there since they took you. Maybe we can use the fact that they were definitely there to track them."

"They *did* track them," Devin said. "All the way back to the gate at the Old Zoo. They've also been talking to Gabriela the whole time I was gone. They've been working with the coven, and with some of the vamps at the club."

Alexis nodded again.

The shower had helped.

She felt like a person again.

But she was also wound almost as tightly as Devin clearly was.

With Devin, she knew it likely had to do with his pack, even more than his obvious upset over Gabriela, and how much he'd clearly distressed her.

But with Devin, it always came back to the pack.

After being separated from his people for so long, she knew he had to be climbing the walls. Every part of his instincts and heart would be screaming at him to get back to them. She knew him well enough to know his alpha thing was an intense thing to have to navigate, even at the best of times. He literally viewed his pack as family.

Not only that, he viewed them as his sole responsibility, the thing that came before absolutely every other person and situation in his life.

Alexis knew the only thing keeping him here, even now, was that Devin viewed The Others and the Red Dragon as the biggest threat his pack currently faced.

But everything in him would be screaming to return to Los Angeles.

Everything in him would be screaming to go to his pack.

It was one thing to not be around them when you were trapped in an alternate dimension... it was something very different to have his people be an airplane flight away, and possibly in danger from whatever the hell Alexis just unleashed on this world. It was far worse to fear they might be in danger of that thing, and not be able to go to them, or get there in time if they needed his help in the flesh.

Alexis touched her thigh in rote at the thought.

There was no knife there, however.

She didn't have any weapons on her person at all.

She couldn't exactly walk around Bangkok with swords strapped to her back, a gun and a whip strapped to her waist, a hunting knife in a sheath on her thigh—not without getting arrested and/or freaking out a hell of a lot of locals.

For the same reason, she had to content herself with bringing a small backpack, which she'd also bought at the airport in Penang. She'd already told Cal they would be putting any weapons and other protective measures they might need in that.

Unzipping the top now, she shoved her whip in it first.

Maybe it was a psychological thing, but she instantly felt better.

She put the sheathed hunting knife in next, maybe

because it had just been on her mind, followed by another, smaller knife, two Glocks and a handful of spare magazines she'd had waiting for her at the hotel safe, and the few hundred U.S. dollars' worth of Thai baht she'd gotten at the Bangkok International Airport.

She'd requested the gun from Gunter, her full-time manager at The White Rabbit, along with the magazines.

Like always, he'd come through.

He'd filled the safe with cash for her, too, but she would leave that here, just in case. She wasn't planning on needing much money where they were going.

Mara, like most supernaturals Alexis contracted with, preferred wire transfers over cash, anyway.

Besides, it was risky walking around with a lot of cash here, even with this kind of arsenal. The guns and knives were risky for other reasons, most of them having to do with Thai law enforcement. If they got caught with guns on the street, they'd likely be labeled terrorists, given that they were foreigners.

Walking around with weapons in any country where she didn't have supernaturals on the police force was risky, though, even when she *did* have access to her magic... and whether the weapon was strapped to her person, or remotely visible at all.

She *would* risk it, of course, given how everything was right now.

But she didn't plan to call attention to herself.

For all she knew, the Red Dragon had tracked them here already, just like he'd tracked them on his home world.

And it wasn't only the more concrete threat of Cal's father.

Other things threatened her, if in a slightly more abstract way.

Things felt... off to her.

That might have been from losing her magic, but Alexis didn't think so.

Even without the magic, things felt… tilted.

She hadn't asked Cal, because she remembered his freak-out at the gate, but she suspected it had something to do with the gates being closed totally.

Inside her, it felt like a coming storm.

She felt on-edge, like a faint electrical current ran over her in some way, pricking the hairs on her arms and the back of her neck, making her feel faintly sick and anxious. Her mind hammered her with questions: whether there had been a price paid by bringing so many through the portal before she closed it, what she'd actually done to this dimension… all the dimensions… by closing the gates in the first place.

Had any of The Others been trapped in here?

What had happened to those dark creatures who had been sent through the gates before, presumably in preparation of taking over this world to utilize it as a primary gate, with her as the last Lightbringer?

What else had been trapped here, with them?

Which gods were here? Which demons?

What other species had been locked behind the closed gates?

Would those who adhered to the Dark, (or those on the Dark-*er* end of the scale) be weakened as much as the Light ones, being cut off from the source of their power?

Or would it only strengthen them?

From what Cal had implied, when he shouted at her by the gate, the Light would fare worse in their isolation from the other planes.

It made her headache worse, her anxiety worse, to contemplate these questions.

Coloring her ability to think about these things, she

increasingly felt an enormous amount of guilt and shame woven in with her nerves.

She hadn't realized she'd stopped getting ready until she grew aware of another presence inside the closet with her.

It wasn't Devin. Devin no longer stood outside the closet door, stressing out with her, sharing the same generalized anxiety without fully acknowledging it.

Devin must have left. He'd likely gone to use the other phone, or maybe to check in with Jules, who'd been talking to her own people in the other room.

In any case, it wasn't either of her best friends.

Cal stood behind her now.

He'd walked in while she'd been lost in her thoughts.

She was dressed, luckily, all but her footwear, but she'd just been standing there, her backpack unzipped on the bureau in front of her as she stared at the closet wall without seeing any of the clothes that hung there.

Cal lightly took hold of her arms, just below her shoulders, and she jumped.

Jerking her head and eyes back, she saw who it was.

She fought to relax.

He kissed the side of her neck, murmuring quietly into her skin.

"You are cut off from the Light too, Lightbringer." He kissed her again, nuzzling her skin with his cheek. "You are reacting to this. You are adjusting. Some part of you is looking for the connections you've lost... just like all of us."

He kissed her again.

She melted into his chest and legs and the heat of his mouth as he kept kissing her. She thought about his words. She felt warmth off him, reassurance, affection... she let herself have all of those things.

She found she didn't want to examine any of it too closely, either.

"You mean the closing of the gates," she said. "You think I'm reacting to that."

"Yes."

"That feels true," she admitted.

Her voice strengthened as she looked back at him.

"Yes," he told her, smiling faintly as he stroked her hair. "You are drawn to me, in part, because of this severing of your usual line to the Ancients. You are trying to find that connection through me... in part because we have shared such a connection in the past."

She thought about that, frowning, and nodded again.

"I see," she said.

He chuckled, stroking her hair, wrapping his hand into it to tug on her with his fingers. She felt a ripple of desire off him. Dense, tangible.

"Do you think my magic left because of that?" she said, closing her eyes as he tugged on her, his arm wrapping around her chest. "Do you think it will come back only after we open the gates?"

He fell silent for a few seconds.

Then he exhaled his held breath.

"I don't know," he admitted. "But I know my father believes it will come back before then."

"Does he?"

"Yes." Cal pressed against her from behind, and again she felt desire on him, mixed with an affection that stole her breath. "He was already thinking about hunting you... about using you... even as he escaped the cavern. As soon as he had reinforcements, he fully intended to come for you, Alexis."

He pressed into her again, closing his eyes.

"Why do you think I 'freaked out,' as you termed it?" he murmured, kissing her neck. "...As you so flatteringly portrayed my fear for you?"

She smiled, rolling her eyes.

Before she could make a remark, he surprised her, wrapping both of his other arm around her. He squeezed her against him in a heat-filled hug, a stronger one than what she'd done to him earlier.

She felt so much longing in that hug, so much heat and desire... she felt it through him so tangibly... it shocked her a little, in spite of herself.

"Yes," he said, again answering a question she hadn't verbalized, or even wondered coherently inside her own mind. "It is likely both of us will be more 'psychic' here, as the humans call it. It is counterintuitive, in a way, but it also makes a kind of sense. When you cannot connect up or down... you will go sideways. It is simply our nature to be connected to something. It is perhaps how we evolved after the last closing of the doors."

Alexis swallowed.

Something about how he said that brought back her fear.

Perhaps because, for the first time, she understood what was at stake.

Maybe for the first time, she *really* understood.

"We must open them before your father does," she said, looking up at him. "That is what you were telling me before. That your father would open the gates in a way that would favor the Dark. That he would try to cause many people... possibly even *most* people... to turn to the Dark to provide that connection, without the Light there to overpower it."

"Yes." Cal nodded. "Definitely."

Alexis felt that sick feeling in her gut worsen.

Cal stroked her face, tracing her jaw.

Even as he did that, he didn't mince words.

"It is highly likely my father would *only* open the portals if he knew he could summon the armies of The Others when he did. I also suspect it is The Others who have some way of overwhelming the gates, so that it is only their connection that comes through."

He gauged her eyes.

"You must realize it's likely they were on the verge of implementing such a thing already. I suspect that would have happened next, once he'd secured control over you on my home world. It is unlikely that killing you was his first plan, but it was definitely on the table. I suspect he will obtain a young Lightbringer to replace you within a few years... assuming he hasn't obtained one for himself already."

Cal's voice grew bitter.

"My father is a big believer in 'training them up young.' He would want control over a being as powerful as a Light-bringer... and from a very young age. He would want to mold them in his image. He would want them completely bound to him. Loyal to him alone. He would want to break them, like he did with Dharma... as he tried to do with me."

Alexis frowned, thinking about that.

"You know what Lightbringers truly are," she said. "You know how we are made."

"Yes."

"Are we really designed, rather than born? Was your father telling the truth about that?"

Cal hesitated, then nodded, giving her an apologetic look.

"It is true," he admitted.

"So he could design one that met his needs?" she said. "Perhaps he wouldn't need to train them at all... he could simply reprogram one of us. Create something with programming he found more malleable. Or more attuned to The Others, perhaps."

There was a silence.

Then Cal nodded reluctantly. "The thought occurred to me. Yes."

Alexis' lips firmed.

She stared at the floor of the closet, then turned, facing him.

"What do you know of *my* programming, Cal?"

She opened her mouth to ask more, but the Traveler held up a hand.

"Perhaps we can speak of this later," he said. "There is much we must discuss. There is the matter of your friend, in that other place…"

He trailed, giving her a warning look.

Alexis felt her chest clench.

Darynda.

Gods, in all of this, she had forgotten her friend. She couldn't think about it now, knowing her thoughts might be heard. Some tiny, whispering part of her couldn't help but think it briefly though, to remember.

Cal said she was still alive, that he and Borghen had somehow made Darynda safe on some other world. Somehow, the two of them also managed to convince the Red Dragon and The Others she was dead.

How had Alexis forgotten?

Cal gave her a harder, even more warning look.

"We will discuss all of it, Lightbringer. In time. When it is safe."

He glanced over his shoulder, focusing briefly on something in the bedroom.

"Right now, however, we do not have that time, my love. If I am reading your devices correctly, our three hours are almost up. And we should not be late to meet this being, from what you told me. That doesn't leave us much travel time… depending on how far this place is."

Frowning, Alexis pulled her phone out of her back pocket, looked at it.

Shit. He was right.

They had fifteen minutes.

"JULES!" she yelled out. "IS THE CAR HERE?"

The half-fae poked her head into the closet.

She glanced surreptitiously at Cal, then focused back on Alexis, her small, white hand gripping the door frame.

She winked at Alexis once she had her attention, lifting her eyebrows rapidly a few times to convey an obvious *hubba-hubba* reference to her and Cal.

Her voice sounded completely normal when she answered Alexis' question, however.

"It's waiting for you. Right outside the lobby doors."

Alexis nodded, even as she glanced at her phone again.

Gods of the Underworld. She must be more out of it than she'd thought.

They would barely make it, even if they left immediately.

Which they most certainly would do.

She zipped up the backpack. Then she leaned down, snatched her boots off the floor of the closet, and brought all of it with her out of the closet and into the other room. She thought about grabbing a jacket, then remembered they were in Bangkok.

Jackets were more or less never necessary here.

She wouldn't take the time to put the boots on inside the hotel room, either.

She'd do that in the hired car.

She swiped a card-key off the side table as she passed, and shoved it in her back pocket, not slowing for the suite's main door.

Cal followed her, not saying a word.

Devin didn't say anything either as he watched her pass… but she swore she could *hear* him grinding his teeth as he glared at the Traveler.

VAMPIRES

*I*t hit her again, how strange she felt, being back in her own dimension.

Some part of her looked for fairies, elves... airships floating outside her car window... those strange, round lights that hovered in the air, illuminating the walls of glass-covered buildings... trees the size of Sequoias growing out of the foundations of houses.

Being in Bangkok might have been less of a shock than going straight back to Los Angeles, but it still required her to adjust her thinking.

It also required her to occasionally remind herself where she was.

More and more, she suspected the real problem might be the closing of the doors.

She was home, but it didn't exactly *feel* like home.

Worse, it felt *less* like home as time passed, not more.

She suspected that was from the Light being cut off from other worlds.

"It is," Cal said.

They had left the car. The two of them now strode down

a street in Old Town, looking at the numbers on doors. Cal strode beside her, wearing black pants that fit his long legs perfectly, along with a dark blue shirt. He looked strangely fresh for Bangkok, even in the humid evening air. If he sweated from the heaviness of that air, Alexis couldn't see it.

Alexis found herself looking at him a lot.

Now, when he confirmed her fears about the effects of the closed portals, she looked at him again.

A part of her would have rather *not* had that confirmed, just yet.

Her responsibility for putting entire universes in danger by closing the portal doors was starting to feel heavy on her too, in a decidedly *different* way than the humid Bangkok air.

Maybe denial would help her push through this better.

In the short term, maybe knowing too much was *not* the answer.

Walking next to her, the Traveler grunted.

Alexis got the sense the grunt was more in sympathy and agreement than it was in derision for her desire for reality-avoidance.

She found the number of the house she was looking for.

She glanced up at the wooden shutters of the old-fashioned, traditional-Thai-style house, noting that the whole thing appeared to be made of teak. It was amazing, really, that no one had ripped the shutters and paneling off the walls.

The wood alone had to be worth a fortune.

Then again, the occupant of the house likely had ways of protecting it. She had, after all, lived on this part of Earth for a few hundred years.

Walking up to the green-painted door, Alexis knocked briskly.

She glanced over her shoulder, and saw Cal take up position behind her, casing the alley to either side.

"There is some field here…" he muttered.

"Yes," she said only.

"I am not familiar with the kind."

Thinking about that, Alexis frowned slightly.

"Do you not have seers on your world?" She tried to remember if she'd ever encountered one in her time there. "You don't, do you? Not even as visitors?"

He pursed his lips.

Hesitating, he seemed to be deciding whether to answer her, even as he answered her.

"No," he said.

Alexis frowned. "There's definitely more to that story than that."

He exhaled in an involuntary-sounding humor.

"There is," he said. "You have a way of asking questions, my love, that inevitably have a long, complicated story behind them."

"Perhaps your world simply has a lot of long, complicated stories, White Dragon," she returned with a raised eyebrow. "It seems the ground is littered with them, whenever I ask even the smallest thing about your world."

He laughed, even as he made a concessionary gesture with one hand.

"Perhaps," he conceded. "I did warn you about that, if you recall."

"You did," she agreed.

Just then, the door opened.

Alexis turned.

She found herself facing an orange-lit opening, in lieu of the green-painted door.

Night had fallen, somewhere in their flying here from Penang, taking a taxi to the hotel, swimming, talking, eating, showering, talking on the phone, dressing again… taking a hired car from the hotel to reach this part of the city. When they drove into Old Town, all of the temples had been lit up, on both sides of the river.

Now, the narrow side-street struck her as dark.

Even with lights on poles across the narrow lane, this house struck her as dark.

She squinted, holding up a hand to see who had opened the door for them.

Whoever they were, they didn't bother to greet her or Cal.

They didn't give them a name, either.

"Come," the low, hissing voice said.

Vampire, Alexis' mind told her.

"Possibly," Cal muttered.

She looked at him, and his lips firmed.

"Possibly a hybrid," he said, shrugging. "Possibly a shifter hybrid."

Alexis frowned. *That is... specific,* she thought at him.

The Traveler King only shrugged again.

Glancing forward, Alexis saw dark red eyes focused on her. It had poked its head out further into the light from the street, so that she could make out the contours and outline of most of its face. She saw the deathly white skin. She saw the creature's nostrils flaring.

Whatever it was, it was obviously smelling her.

No, Alexis thought at Cal. *I'm definitely going with VAMPIRE for this one.*

"Suit yourself," the Traveler King murmured. "But vampires are just so *boring.*"

Alexis stifled a low snort.

She knew it was at least partly wound-up nerves.

The vampire's eyes darted to Cal, then back to her, obviously noticing her attempts not to smile, or laugh in its face.

From the way it looked at her, it definitely heard what Cal said.

It might have even picked up on the fact that she'd answered him without speaking out loud.

All of that still told Alexis "vampire."

Especially the smelling part.

She'd been told by several vampire acquaintances and employees at the Red Whip that Lightbringers tasted significantly more yummy to their kind than the standard human fare.

Thinking about that, Alexis remembered something else.

The one breed of supernatural that tasted *better* to vampires than Lightbringers was seers.

Next to her, Cal grunted.

"Seems a poor choice of house-pet, then."

I think it's more complicated than that, Alexis thought back. *From what I've been told, seers get addicted to getting fed on by vamps. They like it. It's sexual for them. I'm pretty sure for the vamps, too.*

Pausing, she added a touch more sharply,

...And stop saying funny things you're thinking out loud, she scolded.

Unable to decide if she was amused or annoyed, she nudged him with an elbow.

You're going to get both of us bit. Or offend our host. Or both.

The White Dragon grunted, but held up his hands in a kind of apology.

Or maybe a gesture of surrender.

He aimed both things at the vampire at the door.

"Apologies, friend," he said. "My mistress informs me I'm being rude."

"He's often rude," Alexis added. "It's nothing personal. He's a Traveler."

If the vampire accepted Cal's apology, or had any idea of what a Traveler was, no flicker of either thing showed on that deathly white face.

After a bare pause, it receded once more into the darkness.

"Come," the creature said.

Alexis and Cal exchanged looks.

Well, that was a bit weird.

Was Cal right about the hybrid thing?

How would Cal even know that? What reason did he have to think the thing guarding Mara's door would be a much more rare variety of creature than a regular vamp? And if the White Dragon didn't have a specific, concrete *reason* for thinking that, what would be the point of walking down those possibilities?

Why would the Traveler King be contemplating a complex answer to a simple question?

A question no one asked?

"You're overthinking, my love," the Traveler murmured.

Alexis tried to decide if she was.

She decided she was.

Still, it was strange how little magic she felt around herself.

All of her internal danger sensors seemed to be clanging alarms inside her mind, making it difficult to think, deafening her.

Shoving all of that aside when the vamp—or whatever it was—retreated back into the Thai house, she clenched her jaw.

Then, doing her best to silence all of it, she stepped forward.

After glancing over her shoulder to make sure the White Dragon followed her...

She followed the beckoning creature into the dark.

THE OTHER SEER

*T*he vampire—or hybrid, or whatever—led them deep within the house.

Once they'd retreated into the small foyer, the creature looked male to Alexis.

Androgynous, but definitely male.

Slight, with a possibly-Thai face that wore dramatically high cheekbones, he had straight black hair, large crystal-colored eyes, and a well-formed mouth. Really, he looked like a Thai movie star, or possibly a fashion model.

He looked like something out of an anime storybook.

He was definitely beautiful, but something about him made Alexis shudder, anyway.

It was the vampire thing.

She was friends with some vamps. She found many of them beautiful.

But something about them, something physical, something both tangible and difficult to pin down, had always disturbed her. For the same reason, she'd never had an affair with one. She'd never done anything sexual with any vampire at all.

She was pretty sure she was unusual in that revulsion.

From the way they spoke about vamps at the Red Whip, they were incredibly popular as sex partners. She was pretty sure most of the employees at The Red Whip had slept with vamps at one time or another, including Jules.

They definitely weren't Alexis' cup of tea.

She stared at this one now, and fought not to grimace.

His eyes, which had flushed deep scarlet when it first opened the door, now morphed back to the cracked-crystal, colorless eyes of a calm, non-hunting vampire.

Or a vampire that wanted you to *think* it was calm and not hunting, at least.

Alexis never fully trusted them to *ever* not be hunting, which was maybe part of her problem with them. In any case, the extreme reaction she had to the entire species, after everything she'd learned about Lightbringers recently, now made her wonder.

She wondered if she'd been programmed to hate vampires.

She wondered if it was somehow part of her genetic wiring, versus some conclusion she'd come to organically, or through her own internal calculations.

"Yes," Cal said from next to her.

She gave him an annoyed look.

He shrugged, holding up his hands.

"Sorry," he murmured. "I apologize profusely, darling. I entirely forgot we were in denial mode still."

She snorted an involuntary laugh, shaking her head.

Then, turning away from him, she focused back on the house.

The lighting inside the foyer and retreating corridors was strange.

Alexis had no trouble distinguishing walls, furniture, even sculptures and other unusual objects well enough to make her way, but everything struck her as dimly lit to a strange degree, and lit in a way she couldn't fully identify.

Was it candlelight? Some strange kind of lightbulb?

Magic?

Seers generally were notable for their *not* employing magic, per se.

Unlike most non-humans living inside Alexis' dimension, the otherworldly "talents" of seers were said to be biological in nature... not supernatural... which could occasionally make them an odd race to deal with.

Ironically or not, for someone like Alexis, who had been trained (...*programmed,* her mind muttered in annoyance...) to deal primarily with supernaturals, seers came off as strangely exotic, even borderline mysterious.

If you asked a seer, seers weren't supernatural at all, really.

They were a different but related species.

They were related to humans, they would say, in particular, but like a fox to a dog, a bear to a wolf.

Of course, seers themselves believed they weren't just "different" to humans, but more advanced, even a more evolved form of humanity. She'd heard them called *homo sarhacienne* by some, but she had no idea what that meant.

"Sarhacienne" wasn't even Latin.

Alexis had been told the word came from the original language spoken by the seer race, which made the whole designation seem... weird.

Why not simply use seer words for both?

Alexis had even heard speculation from some seers that their race came from the future. Or, conversely, that it came from the far past. She'd also heard a theory that humans were imported into the current dimensions from disconnected time dimensions where they hadn't yet evolved into the psychic abilities of their seer "cousins."

A lot of it struck her as pure species-ism, frankly.

Many seers themselves seemed to view it the same.

Alexis had noticed that the more polite among the seer race didn't voice the origins of their species in those terms, as part of a hierarchy, or some twisted evolutionary timeline.

Alexis heard more than a few rants from the less-polite ones, however, lecturing her on the fact of seer superiority and the dangers of "prehistoric" human nature.

Whenever she brought up magic, the seers inevitably bristled.

They would remind her again that they were not "super-natural" but "advanced."

Truthfully, most of it struck Alexis as a matter of semantics.

The biological "gifts" of seers sure seemed like magic to her.

Moreover, seers acknowledged many aspects of the magical world.

They seemed to fully experience those things as "real."

They knew all about the portal gates.

Alexis often thought seers understood those gates better than anyone.

Mara herself told Alexis that seers were just as dependent on their connections to other worlds as the most magick-y of the magicked supernaturals. They operated most of their powers in a non-physical space they called "The Barrier," which had some relationship to the portals.

Moreover, they talked of creatures both "Dark" and "Light," as well as "soul aberrations" among their own kind that created exceedingly rare shapeshifter and telekinetic seers. They talked about Dark beings they categorized as "non-corporeal" seers, and to Alexis, those creatures sounded a hell of a lot like wizards or magicians, or even demons.

Truthfully, they were a proud, often arrogant... sometimes full-blown *racist*... race, one that might even view its powers as "natural" as a kind of snobbery against what they saw as the "woo-woo" magics of other races.

In a sense, claiming their own nature as biology-based was a way of flexing with beings whose powers they saw as less-than, or even frivolous.

Alexis didn't much care.

The politics of the various races mostly bored her.

And really, she didn't much care what seers called themselves, either, or whether they defined their powers as "magic" or "science."

In functional terms... apart from reproduction, perhaps... she didn't see a lot of difference.

Even with reproduction, there seemed to be non-physical variations and anomalies even among seers. Seers themselves usually claimed those differences had more to do with past lives and the interference of Barrier beings than the genetics of the biological parents.

Then again, perhaps Alexis simply didn't understand it.

Like gods, seers generally weren't her problem.

They weren't a race that seemed to concern itself much with the portals.

Well... not until now.

The three of them reached the end of the twisting corridor.

Alexis followed the beautiful, young-looking vampire into a high-ceilinged room, seemingly made entirely of teak wood. All of it shone with the same old-looking sheen: walls, floors, window shutters that had been flung open to the night, built-in cabinets and shelves, tables and other pieces of free-standing furniture. For a few seconds as Alexis looked around, she only saw the same, warm-colored wood.

Then she picked out a black leather couch.

Paintings.

A lacquer-covered table, decorated with strange animals and human-like figures took up the very center of the room. The images dancing across its surface included dragons, what looked like knights and water-nymphs, kings and queens, mythical animals she didn't recognize, a giant tortoise holding up what looked like a painting of the world.

She saw the seer herself a beat later, mostly because she turned her head, staring at them from where she sat in a red-painted chair beside one of the open windows.

Before she turned her head, Mara had been staring out at a small canal where a boat motored by, darting past a line of trees and flowering bushes.

Her appearance was striking, as was that of most seers.

Long, dark-auburn hair flowed down her shoulders and back, looked possibly dyed.

With the strange, not-human ethnicities of seers, it was impossible to say for sure where she'd come from, assuming she'd come from this Earth at all. Her face somehow managed to look both Asian and not-Asian at the same time.

Her pale-green eyes with the dark brown rings around the irises shone in the light of candles that lit different parts of the room.

She was beautiful, and definitely not-human in appearance.

Her high cheekbones were somehow too high.

Her jaw was somehow too well-defined, her lips too well-formed.

Her expression remained too still, yet her eyes somehow too expressive.

Her eyes also seemed to contain some fragment of light, something that didn't come from anything in the room.

Something about all of it struck Alexis as feeling frozen in time.

The room, the teak wood shutters, the canal, the palm trees and flowers.

The seer herself.

The seer looked at her, Alexis, and then at Cal.

Frowning a tiny bit at the sight of Cal, she eventually looked at the vampire who led them into this part of the house. After a bare hesitation, she nodded, indicating the vampire could leave her alone with her two houseguests.

The beautiful, deathly white creature, who looked time-less in a whole different way, receded back into the darkness of the corridor.

Mara looked back at Alexis and Cal.

Alexis folded her arms, waiting for the seer to speak, knowing it was likely the seer was reading her mind, still deciding how much to trust her.

She'd lost patience, and decided to be the first to break the silence after all, when a voice came from above them, seemingly from the ceiling, making Alexis jump about a foot.

"Why did you close the portals?"

The voice wasn't Mara's.

It wasn't female, either.

A deep, heavy-sounding voice, it resonated through the open spaces between floor and ceilings, vibrating the teak walls.

It didn't sound angry, or accusing, or even worried.

It sounded genuinely curious… like he wished to know the answer to his question, nothing more.

"You said you needed her," the male voice prompted. "… My mate."

It said the last word with a significantly harder touch of emphasis.

"Why?" the male said. "Why did you need her?"

Alexis had found him with her eyes by the time the male fell silent.

The high-ceilinged room had a library loft, and he stood on the level above, looking down at them, his hands resting on the railing in front of several tall stacks of books.

When Alexis didn't immediately speak, he began strolling across the walkway at the end of the rows, making his way to a staircase at Alexis' right. She followed him with her eyes as he reached the top of the stairs and began walking down.

Long, gray-streaked hair had been pulled back from his angular face with a wooden clasp.

His pale, deep-set, violet-colored eyes fixed on hers.

He wore an odd scar across his face, a diagonal, white-cut line that looked old, that marred his features, but without making him ugly or unattractive, per se. The thick scar ran from his lips all the way to below one of his eyes, giving his face a deathly serious, and somewhat dangerous look.

Like a pirate, her mind muttered.

If he'd been human, she would have pegged him at roughly late fifties, early sixties.

A handsome, dignified man, edging into the older part of middle age.

But seers lived a lot longer than humans.

From the little she knew, he could easily be closer to five hundred years old.

In seer years, fifty was basically an adolescent.

Replaying his words in her mind, she met his gaze.

Her eyebrow rose as one piece of information hit her a little late.

"Mate?" she said politely. She glanced at Mara, then back at him. "I did not realize Mara had a mate. I apologize for not knowing how to address you—"

"Varlan," the older seer said. "My name is Varlan."

He had nearly reached the floor.

Alexis waited for him to reach it, then unfolded her arms.

"I am Alexis—" she began.

"I know who you are." The older seer gaze at her unblinkingly. "Tell me what you want from us. Tell me why you called my mate for help. Tell me the truth... although I will discern it regardless." His gaze swiveled to Cal. "From both of you."

Alexis believed him.

She didn't even think about how or why at first.

His words definitely didn't feel like an empty boast.

Moreover, that time, Alexis heard the warning in his words.

She glanced at Cal, who stared at the gray-haired seer, his expression alert, verging on wary. She found herself thinking that Cal saw in this seer what she saw.

Infiltrator, they used to call them.

Many seers who had been trained as infiltrators also worked as occasional assassins, even full-blown contract killers.

Something about this male seer, who continued to stare at them, his expression as still as blank stone, made her think he could have been one of those seers.

Everything about him struck her as disarmingly, deceptively inconspicuous, like the opposite of bluster or posturing.

It came through as something more akin to camouflage.

The stillness of his eyes, the micro-expressions flickering across his angular features, even the scar he wore... everything about him and his demeanor, really, suggested to Alexis that the male seer was dangerous.

He was far more dangerous than he seemed to be trying to appear.

He was a dire wolf pretending to be a golden retriever.

"Tell me what you want from my mate," Varlan repeated. "Tell me now."

Alexis nodded, feeling her jaw harden.

She adjusted her feet unconsciously, adopting a more wide-legged, verging-on-aggressive stance, even though it felt more defensive than otherwise.

"We hoped we might obtain her services for tracking," Alexis said, glancing at Mara before looking back at the taller male. "We were forced to close the portals, as you said—"

"We?" Cal muttered.

Alexis glanced at him, then conceded the point.

"*I* did it. I decided to take that step on my own," she amended. "It felt like there was little choice at the time. However, we brought a being through the portal with us when we came. A Traveler..." Again, she glanced at Cal, then looked back at the male seer. "...Not this one. A far more dangerous one, with an agenda against our world."

"Why?" Varlan's voice remained emotionless. "Why would you bring such a being here? Knowing it was dangerous to this dimension?"

"It was a decision we made. Perhaps a mistake. In any case, he is a..."

She hesitated, seeking words.

"...I guess you could say, a malevolent personality," she finished. "He will try to re-open the portals before we are able to do it. He will try to control the gates, letting things into this dimension that no being of integrity would want. Worse, he would seek to do this while blocking the Light connected to beings of goodwill who still reside here."

Varlan frowned.

The way he did it, Alexis felt an urge to explain more, to tell him more.

She suppressed that urge, biting her lip as she re-folded her arms.

There was a silence while they stared at one another.

She found herself a hundred percent certain he was reading her.

She glanced at Mara, then back at the male.

Clearly, Mara intended for him to speak for both of them.

In any case, Mara focused minutely on the male, as well.

When Varlan didn't say anything more at first, or immediately ask more questions, Alexis stood there, shifting her weight from foot to foot. She was just trying to decide whether she should break the silence herself, when the older seer finally did so.

Clicking in a low, strangely melodious fashion, he shook his head.

He walked over to where Mara sat by the window.

He reached for her, stroking the back of his mate's neck with his fingers.

He looked at Cal, then at Alexis.

"I understand," he said simply.

His voice grew lower, more ominous.

"I am familiar with The Others."

Sighing a bit, he added, "I am, sadly, far more familiar with them than either of you could possibly know. I have known them called by a different name. Several different names, in fact. But they are always the same. They always want the same things."

Seeming to see the frown that came to Alexis' face, Varlan waved a graceful hand in her direction. It appeared to be a dismissive gesture, although it contained a nuance she found fascinating.

She watched his fingers glide in intricate patterns through the air much as she'd watched Cal's body go from smoke to flesh and back to smoke and light.

"It would take too long to explain in detail," Varlan continued, preempting her questions. "Although I will give you a shorter version, since what happened to me is relevant to what interests you most about The Others now."

Pausing, gauging both of their eyes, he went on in the same voice.

"I have fallen through portals, as well, my very young cousins," he said gravely. "Before the Lightbringers were made. Back at the beginning of the current historical period, when the portals re-opened. We, meaning my people, the seers, call that time the last Displacement. We view it as the beginning of a new cycle of evolution."

Cal frowned.

So did Alexis.

They exchanged looks.

"That was thousands of years ago," Cal muttered.

"Technically... yes." Varlan looked at him. "But it was far longer ago than you perhaps think. It was not *only* thousands of years ago... it was thousands *upon thousands* of years ago, my young friend. I do not know the exact number, but I know the Dreng... those beings you call The Others... were cut off from all the other worlds."

He paused, as if thinking.

"Neither of you fully understand your own history," he said, looking between her and Cal once more. He clasped his hands at the base of his back. "Or the history of your races. But that is not important now... and this does not strike me as the best time or place to explain it. Suffice it to say, the dimensions I traversed were not simply different alternate versions of the same timelines. I skipped over... and eventually traversed the timeline itself. It was an aberration. One might even call it a mistake. I do believe in mistakes... but I recognize just how unusual this is, even in such an extraordinary time."

His strangely perfect mouth hardened perceptibly.

He looked at Mara.

As soon as he did, the male seer's violet eyes softened.

He caressed her cheek with his fingers.

"I believe there are reasons for this," he said softly.

She smiled up at him, leaning her face into his palm.

Something at her smile struck Alexis as taut.

She wondered just how much the closed portals affected them.

Looking at Mara's face, at the tension in her features, Alexis found herself thinking it was likely a lot. She'd never seen Mara look so pale.

Varlan turned to her, Alexis, his eyes shrewd, like he'd heard her.

Then he looked between her and Cal.

"Suffice it to say… I traversed time. A lot of time."

Varlan continued to stroke Mara's neck, but his eyes looked distant once more.

"I do not know what happened at the end of my old world. I know what I was told happened, what was passed down in mythology and historical texts over the millennia since. More than that, I know the doors were opened again. When they were, The Dreng were barred from entry. They were left behind, on that dying world. They were trapped somehow. The rest of the worlds were made safe from them."

Varlan's voice turned grim.

"I suppose there are no permanent states… good or bad." He met Alexis' gaze. "Somehow, The Dreng… The Others… have escaped. They are no longer imprisoned on the dead world on which my people left them."

Alexis frowned.

Again, she looked at Cal.

Cal quirked an eyebrow in return, but Alexis definitely didn't get the sense Cal didn't believe the old seer.

Alexis didn't disbelieve him either, even though his words sounded fantastical.

Was Varlan really saying he had been alive when the doors were closed the last time? And was he really intimating that what had happened to his world, his dimension, all those thousands of years ago... was he saying that might happen again here?

Did that mean he knew what would happen next?

Did he know whether she would be able to re-open the gates? Did he know whether that would help them or hurt them?

The seer seemed to hear her.

He smiled. There was no humor in the smile.

It didn't in any way reach his eyes.

"The stories were not exaggerated," he said. "The world I come from... it was a dark world. Darker than this one. It had been cut off from the portals... most of the portals, at least... for millennia."

He paused, sighing in a strange sort of clicking purr.

"We were trapped in the darkness with the Dreng. They cut us off from much of the Light. We lived in a world that they more or less ruled."

Cal and Alexis exchanged looks.

As they did, Alexis felt a harder knot forming in her belly.

THE WAYS OF SEERS

"**W**ell, this is all very fascinating," Cal said, his voice dry.

He managed to say it in a way that conveyed his belief that the old seer with the gray-streaked hair was definitely, without doubt, batshit crazy.

Alexis quirked an eyebrow at him.

She wasn't fooled—any more than the old seer likely was fooled.

Alexis heard the harder, denser note under the lighter, emptier voice Cal used on the surface. Cal might wish to *pretend* he thought Varlan crazy. Even more likely, Cal probably wished he really, truly believed the seer to be crazy... but he didn't.

Cal believed Varlan's words, even though he didn't want to.

When Alexis glanced at Varlan, the seer gave her a barely-perceptible nod.

Clearly, he agreed with her assessment.

Alexis couldn't decide how she felt about that, either.

About Varlan reading her.

About Varlan seeing into Cal so easily.

About her *own* ability to see past Cal's mask.

About Varlan letting her know what he saw openly like that.

She found herself tempted to tell Varlan to leave Cal's mind the hell alone, to stay away from the Traveler, and to stay away from her mind, too.

She understood Cal's bluster.

She understood Cal's reluctance to believe the old seer, because she felt it herself.

But really, what bothered her most was how connected she felt to the Traveler King, how strangely possessive, even protective she felt of him. She honestly couldn't decide if it reassured her or alarmed her, how easily she saw past the mask Caliginous wore so much of the time. Or how much it bothered her that Varlan could clearly do the same.

Varlan snorted, clearly hearing her.

When Alexis turned to stare at the old seer, he lifted his eyebrow.

She saw a faint warmth in his eyes as he smiled at her that time. His violet eyes flickered to Cal, then back to her. Alexis couldn't fail to see the knowing look that lived there.

She didn't want to read into that look, so she chose not to.

Varlan snorted a second time.

His amusement with both of them was plain.

Cal pretended to hear none of it.

"...It truly is fascinating," the Traveler King repeated, not so much as glancing at Alexis herself. "Hearing about time jumps, ancient evils, exploding worlds, the imminent end of ours. But it's not exactly *useful* for us right now, is it? It's not going to help us *stop* The Others in what they plan to do?"

His jaw hardened.

That time, he spared a glance at Alexis.

His now-golden eyes swiveled back to Varlan.

"We came to you for *help*. In a very real and *immediate* area of concern, cousin. In short, we need your assistance in tracking someone. Someone dangerous, with whom I would hope you did not wish to give the task of re-opening the portal doors."

"We can assist with that, of course," Varlan said.

His words came through calm, polite, even as he gave a subtle bow of the head.

"Of course we will assist," he added. "If it is the being who followed you through the doors, the one who shares a light connection to you and your wife... I have tracked that person already. I can tell you exactly where he is."

There was a silence.

"What?" Cal stared at the male seer, his eyes morphing from that pale gold to a harder, darker amber. "You have known his location all this time?"

"I don't know about 'all this time,'" Varlan replied calmly. "But I made a point of locating every person and every *thing* that went through the doors with you from that other world. The planet your wife calls 'The Traveler World' when she thinks about it, but for which you have a different name your mind."

Pausing, Varlan tilted his head, as if listening to a faraway sound.

"...Lakrias. *Na?* Do I have that correctly?"

Cal frowned.

He looked at Alexis, then back at the seer.

"Yes," he said, his voice blunt. "That is what it is called."

"Where is he?" Alexis blurted.

When they both looked at her, she firmed her mouth, folding her arms as she frowned at the gray-haired seer. She looked at Mara, then back at him.

"The Red Dragon. Our lost Traveler. Is he still in Asia?"

"Yes." Varlan's facial expression appeared unmoved by her more aggressive stance, but Alexis watched the seer as he placed himself more squarely between her and Mara. "He is still here. I saw him heading this way, in fact. Towards Bangkok. From what I could feel, he is currently on a boat, coming up the coast of Thailand. He has several others with him now."

"Others?" Alexis frowned.

Varlan nodded, once, seer-fashion.

As he did, he made one of those odd hand gestures unique to seers.

Alexis was fairly certain that particular gesture meant "yes."

"Human?" she pressed.

"I think they are more his kind," Varlan said, aiming a jerked jaw towards Cal. "The one you call Red Dragon found them outside the mountain where you all came through the portal."

Varlan paused as Cal gave Alexis a grim look.

The look didn't say *I told you so,* but something damned close.

Maybe more along the lines of, *I told you, right? That's exactly what I told you, when I tracked him out of the cave.*

Then the middle-aged seer looked between them.

After a longer-feeling pause, he went on in a darker voice.

"He knows where you are. He is tracking you. Specifically *you,* Lightbringer."

The seer nodded, once, at Alexis that time.

"He is also thinking very intensely about opening the gates," Varlan added grimly. "So yes, I suspect you are right about his intentions here. He seems determined to control whatever frequencies of Light and Dark are allowed into this dimension. Possibly all the dimensions, but definitely this one, as a start."

Alexis and Cal exchanged another set of grim looks.

Then Cal's mouth hardened, right before his stare jerked back to Varlan.

"We need a way to open the doors back up again, friend. Can you help us with that? It is really the only way we have to deal with…"

He bit his lip, silencing himself briefly.

It dawned on Alexis that he'd been about to name his father. Clearly, he didn't particularly want to admit to Varlan that the Traveler they sought *was* his biological father.

"…the other Traveler my wife told you of," Cal continued, his voice a touch harder. "We must open the gates before he is able to do so. Unfortunately, this Traveler is versed in the occult systems employed and taught on many worlds. He has made a study of these things… for decades."

His mouth turned more grim.

"…Possibly centuries. For the same reason, it is likely he has a better understanding of how to re-open the portals than we do."

Alexis refolded her arms.

For some reason, hearing him call her his wife here, in front of Mara and Varlan, on her version of Earth, felt a lot different than when he'd used that word on his own world, or even in the hotel room with the others.

She'd caught Varlan using the same word, of course.

With Varlan, it felt more like probing.

Varlan might even have been needling the two of them, looking for a reaction, most likely to discern more information.

Something about the way Cal said it struck her as more matter-of-fact.

Hell, he sounded almost *sincere* when he used it now.

She didn't detect any sarcasm or attempts to push her buttons at all, not anymore.

Not for the first time, she wondered exactly how Cal really did see the two of them, not just right now, but in the long term.

Varlan blinked.

He glanced at Mara. A smile formed on the edges of Mara's lips, right before she shook her head perceptibly, rolling her eyes perceptibly, too.

Alexis didn't want to ask.

Even so, she was reasonably sure they were laughing at her and Cal.

Cal likely caught it, too.

His voice sharpened.

"Can you help us?" he said. "Can you help us open the gates? Or are you just amusing yourselves right now? Leading us around like fools?"

Varlan looked away from his wife.

He met Cal's gaze, his own unmoving.

"I would offer some advice," he said, his voice serious. "If it were me, I would not waste my time trying to track your Traveler father, King Caliginous. You are right about him. He is quite insane... and utterly single-minded in his goals. If you focus your attention on tracking him down, you will only be forced to kill him. It is best to assign others that task."

Varlan looked politely at Alexis.

"Perhaps your friends, Lightbringer? The werewolf? Or possibly his entire pack, if you were able to bring them here?"

Exhaling in another of those clicking sighs, Varlan gestured subtly with a hand out towards the canals.

"Perhaps it would be easier to hire local help, rather than transporting so many here. In Bangkok, vampires tend to be the most common supernaturals... as you no-doubt know, Alexis Poole. You could hire and enlist such vampires to track and deal with the Red Dragon for you, via your club. I have a few I could lend you, as well. They would work for reasonable wages. And they are loyal to myself... and to my wife."

Alexis felt her irritation ebb slightly.

Thinking about his offer, she nodded a beat later.

It was a good suggestion.

It made sense to her—especially in regard to leaving her and Cal out of the part where Cal might be faced with the choice of whether or not he should kill his father.

Again.

She gave a short bow, executing it seer-fashion, as she had been taught.

"I thank you for the offer, cousin. Your suggestion is a logical one."

She looked at Cal, hesitating.

"...Of course, the disposition of his father is entirely the decision of the current Traveler King," she said next. "For the same reason, I must discuss it with him, before we commit to a course. But I will cover any costs or fees to your people, if he decides to go this route."

She hesitated again, watching Cal.

She couldn't read his expression at all that time.

Well, not in terms of what he wanted to do with his father.

She had no idea if he'd decided to kill the old man or not.

She looked back at Varlan, firming her jaw.

"The more pressing matter is the gates," she added.

The old seer nodded, once.

"The more pressing matter is the gates," Varlan agreed.

"Do you know how to open them?"

Varlan's lips toyed with a smile. "Myself? Personally?"

"Yes."

Varlan continued to look at her for a few beats, in that unnerving, overly-staring way of seers. Then he let out a slow, purring sigh. Giving his head a barely-perceptible shake, he let out a deeper version of that great-cat purr.

"No," he said. "I do not."

"How did it happen last time?" Cal said, speaking from Alexis' other side.

Varlan glanced at Cal.

After a bare pause, he made one of those graceful shrugs of the hand.

"I do not know that, either. I was gone from that world by then. I had already been thrown into an unstable portal." Varlan paused, looking only at Cal. "But I do know, the beings who managed it destroyed their world in order to accomplish their goal."

The silence deepened.

Then Cal let out a choking, disbelieving kind of laugh.

Varlan spoke before it could turn into words.

"Those beings are not available to aid you now," the older seer warned. "As I said, that was thousands upon thousands of years ago now. Unless they were thrown into a time portal like me, they are obviously dead. At least within the material realms. Even if they were not, I have my doubts you could even get them here… and even more doubts that they would help you, if you could. They would view it as an abuse of their powers, I suspect."

He smiled faintly, as if the thought amused him.

That amusement came with another faraway stare, as if the old seer were remembering something, or possibly someone.

Whatever he remembered, something about it definitely amused him.

When the silence stretched too long, Cal cleared his throat.

"Any thoughts on a Plan B?" the White Dragon said. "Preferably one that doesn't involve *destroying the entire planet*... or dimension... or whatever it was that last time... and result in all of our deaths?"

Cal motioned towards Mara, without taking his eyes off the older male.

"I imagine that would put a dent in your life here. Wouldn't it, Mr. Varlan?"

There was another silence.

Mara smiled, drawing Alexis' eyes.

"It's just Varlan," she said calmly. "There is no 'Mister' among seers. We have never used such titles. He is only Varlan. Unless you wish to know his clan name, as well."

Cal frowned. He opened his mouth to speak.

Alexis strongly got the impression most of those words would have been curse words, if he'd been allowed to proceed.

But before Cal could let loose, Mara raised a hand.

Her voice grew a touch warning.

"...And there is no reason to yell at my husband, King Caliginous. We will help you as much as we possibly can."

"Then tell us who to go to," Alexis said, blunt, focusing only on Mara. "If you cannot open the gates yourselves, and the last beings who tried destroyed the world and imprisoned The Others, then why would the Red Dragon think it can be done? Who will he go to, in order to accomplish this?"

There was another silence.

In it, Mara and Varlan exchanged looks.

Again, Alexis saw the taut look rise to Mara's face, right before she nodded.

It struck Alexis just how pale the female seer appeared, and how odd that was.

Was Mara sick?

Before she could wonder about this long, Varlan broke the silence.

"It is the Dark Gods you want," the gray-haired male said.

"Only they can help you re-open the portals. And only if they decide they want to."

"How would we ask them?" Cal asked, his voice taut.

"*You* do not ask them anything," Varlan said, giving him a faintly dismissive look. "They won't speak to you, cousin."

His pale, light-filled eyes settled flatly on Alexis.

"They will speak only to the Lightbringer," he said. "And then only if they want to, as I said. It is equally possible they will refuse to speak to either of you... or anyone in your party. Or anyone in this dimension, for that matter..."

Cal glanced at Alexis, frowning.

She noticed only then that he'd stepped in front of her.

The way he stood there, it struck her as *almost* like how Varlan had stood between them and Mara.

It felt different though, on Cal.

Not only did his stance feel protective in the physical sense, but Alexis sensed something more there. It felt almost like Cal didn't want Varlan in Alexis' head any more than Alexis wanted Varlan in Cal's. Somehow, looking at where he stood, how he stood, she realized the gesture had been done out of fear for her.

These seers scared him for some reason.

At the very least, they ignited some kind of aggression in him.

Alexis met his gaze, more or less mirroring his faint frown.

Then they both looked back at the two seers, their eyes shifting simultaneously.

"What are the Dark Gods?" Alexis asked.

13

NOW WHAT?

"*W*ell, that was utterly and ridiculously maddening," Cal muttered.

He lengthened his already-long strides, making his way down the uneven sidewalk.

He glanced at her only briefly, seemingly to reassure himself she continued to pace him as they navigated the crowded streets of Old Town Bangkok.

It was fully dark out now, but lights shone all around them.

Lanterns hung from the old buildings along the street.

Bars emitting music and laughter dotted the alleys and smaller lanes they passed, along with restaurants, clothing stalls, tables covered in handmade jewelry and knick-knacks, live animals performing tricks.

Hawkers sold everything from fried, black spiders tourists could eat on a lark, T-shirts saying "I got Banged in Bangkok," fried spring rolls and Pad Thai, stalls with Tom Yum soup and fried shrimp. Fake holy relics covered still more display tables, mostly in the form of pendants people wore on their person to ward off evil spirits or attract good luck.

Alexis wove through the thick foot-traffic next to Cal, surrounded by the smells of sweat and alcohol and sweet chili and fried shrimp.

She fought to think about what came next, as they aimed for the river, with its lit-up temples, known locally as *wats,* in the distance.

Through the gaps in the buildings, she glimpsed one of the more famous of those wats jutting up above the water. It stood on the other side of the river from where they walked, accented by blue and green spotlights and surrounded by palm trees.

Boats and ferries puttered past the front of it with their smoke-belching diesel engines. Tourists gawked from the inside of the windowless boats, snapping photos of all the old buildings, but especially *Wat Arun,* or Temple of the Dawn.

Normally, she liked Bangkok.

She sometimes even liked the seedier, touristy parts of Bangkok, like this.

Today, however, looking around at the stumbling drunk tourists and the more knowing, cynical looks exchanged by vendors and *tuk-tuk* drivers, all of it struck her as vaguely ominous.

To the people living here, nothing had changed.

To Alexis, however, it felt like the world had already slowly begun to burn. Someone had lit the match, and now they all waited for the fire to find them, for the heat to grow hotter and spread, until it could no longer be avoided.

They were running out of time.

She could feel it.

Even without what the seers had told her, she likely would have felt it.

Varlan, who made it clear he'd seen at least one apocalypse already, clearly thought something bad was coming.

She could feel what he felt, without even really knowing what "it" was.

Cal looked at her, his expression grim.

"Yes," he said.

"You feel it? What I was thinking?"

"Yes." His mouth briefly pursed. "Although it worries me much more that *you* can feel it, Lightbringer. In myself, I could possibly dismiss it as paranoia or even trauma from my father... but you were put here *explicitly* to sense such things. You were tasked with protecting your assigned dimension from the encroachment of Darkness."

She didn't have an answer for that.

Apparently, Cal didn't either.

He didn't elaborate beyond what he'd already said.

But then, he didn't really need to.

"What did you think of it?" he said next. "What they told us? About the Dark Gods? Do you get any intuitions about this?"

Alexis frowned.

A sharp laugh jerked her eyes to the left, making her tense.

She glanced over at a drunken twenty-something, who threw her head back and cackled a second time, gripping a coconut in one hand, a lime green straw coming out the cut-off top. Whatever lived inside that coconut husk, Alexis figured it had to be around eighty proof.

She forced herself to relax, including her grip on the backpack.

Clearly, all of her *fight* instincts were fully triggered.

"I don't know what I think," she said truthfully. "About the Dark Gods, or about anything he said. There was something strange there. Not just with him. With Mara, too."

Still thinking, she added,

"But we have nothing else. Right? What else do we have? We at least must investigate the small bit they gave us, don't you think?"

Cal frowned.

Then, sighing, he gave her a sideways look.

"I suppose we must," he admitted with a graceful flourish. "You are right that we have nothing else. We have *absolutely nothing* apart from this to follow. So we follow it. At least until that changes. Maybe it will shake something else loose."

He lifted an eyebrow, giving her a wan smile.

"It will keep us occupied while others hunt my father, at least."

Alexis agreed.

The seers told them only a very small number of beings had the "punch" to re-open the gates, or even to re-open communication with the Ancients.

The specific type of seer from that other world, the ones who had opened the gates the last time, didn't exist on this one, apparently. Some form of "super-seer," they hadn't come to this dimension at all, at least not as far as Varlan knew.

The beings that *were* here, in this dimension, Varlan and Mara didn't seem to know much about, either.

They called them "Dark Gods."

Alexis wasn't exactly sure what that meant, but Cal seemed to know.

"Yes," the Traveler said next to her.

"You know what they are?"

Cal thought about that.

Then he exhaled, seemingly in frustration. "No. Not exactly. But I have *heard* of them. This is not the first time I've been made aware of their existence. My father spoke of them. When I was a child. He held rituals to attempt to harness their powers for his own ends... back before he got delusions of destroying entire life cycles," he added wryly.

Giving her a more serious look, he added,

"Back then, he mostly wanted his grudges addressed against other species. Ones he had declared enemies to the Travelers. Later, it was against his domestic enemies, too. Then it was against much larger groups of beings… basically anyone not under his control. You can likely see where it developed from that."

Alexis thought about his words.

She focused on whether they might help her and Cal now.

"Was he ever successful?" she asked. "In using their powers for his own ends?"

Cal exhaled, sounding almost tired.

"I honestly don't know. He often lied about such things."

"What do you *think?*" she pressed. "Could he have pulled such a thing off?"

There was a silence.

Then Cal gave her a hard look.

"I think he may have been *somewhat* successful… in a limited way, at least in a few small ways. But I don't know if he accomplished that with the aid of the Dark Gods, specifically. Demons, sure. Dark magicians and warlocks, sure."

Cal's jaw firmed as he thought.

"As for the Dark Gods themselves… I do think it's *possible* he managed to contact them. He might have even secured a favor or two from such beings. But my guess is, his attempts to use them in any *directed* way remained in their infancy, at least while he retained the throne."

He gave her a grim look.

Pursing his lips, he added,

"He obviously didn't have such powerful beings at his beck and call while he held the throne… or he never would have been deposed. I know part of the punishment against him, when he was first imprisoned, was to cut him off from use of any of his magics."

Alexis nodded absently when he finished.

She continued to think through his words, frowning faintly.

"Can you track them?" she asked next. "Can you find these Dark Gods yourself?"

She'd asked the seers the same question, and they'd said no.

But if Cal's father knew how to find them, and Cal's father had a connection to Cal, then it stood to reason that Cal could possibly use his father to—

"They aren't really those sorts of beings," Cal cut in cryptically.

She frowned. "What sorts of beings?"

"The *tracking* sorts of beings," the Traveler told her.

Alexis stepped around a group of tourists sitting on the curb. The four of them shared a few plates of food between them as they drank Chang beer in oversized cans: shrimp rolls with sweet chili, pork skewers, fried rice, mango and sticky rice, papaya slices.

"What kind of beings are they?" she said next. "If not the tracking sort?"

"I have no idea. But not the kind you can track by normal means."

His jaw firmed again as he thought.

After a few seconds, Cal shrugged.

"If they were," he added. "The seers could have done it… especially that gray-haired one, who struck me as not only old, but highly-trained. They wouldn't have sent us to some local sorceress to have her conjure them up for us."

He clenched his jaw.

When he next spoke, his voice sounded worried.

"I'm guessing they are right," he admitted. "A ritual is likely the way to go here, Lightbringer. Spells. Castings. Possibly a séance of some kind. We're better off going to the sorceress. Or finding some other witch… someone with a decent command of light *and* dark magic. Or a vampire with similar credentials. Or a warlock."

He aimed a grim look at her.

"I think we need to find someone who can open a line of communication using blood or earth magicks, in particular… possibly even fae magic, if your friend Jules has a line on someone like that here in Bangkok. Maybe we need to organize an old-fashioned conjuring… or summoning… or even a sacrifice."

At her disbelieving look, he held up a hand.

"Not a *person*," he clarified. "I was thinking a bull or something. Possibly a goat. Or a chicken. Around here, I don't know… maybe a big lizard. Or a monkey."

Alexis frowned.

It made sense, but still, everything about this felt dangerous as hell.

"I agree," Cal said. "I strongly suspect these beings aren't exactly on the side of the 'Light,' or we could find a less savory way of calling on their help. Then again, if they were of the Light, my father likely wouldn't have gone to them for help in the first place."

His frown deepened.

"…Which means, of course, they're as likely to kill us as help us. But from what those seers said, we don't have much choice."

Alexis felt a coldness in her chest at his words.

She took that to mean some part of her Lightbringer nature agreed with him.

Unfortunately, it agreed with him on pretty much all of it.

"So you think we should go to the sorceress first?" she said. "The name Mara gave us. We should start there, right?"

Cal frowned.

"I don't know," he said. "I suppose. Mara didn't seem all

that sure about them. If I didn't know better, I would have thought Varlan *forced* her to give us that name… likely to get rid of us. She didn't seem very keen to give it to us on her own."

Alexis' mouth tightened more.

She agreed with that, too.

In fact, she'd strongly gotten the impression Mara gave them the name reluctantly, possibly under the urging of Varlan, as Cal thought. Perhaps it was simply the only person they knew in Bangkok who operated the right kind of magic.

Perhaps Mara knew more about the Dark Gods than she'd let on.

In any case, given Mara's reaction to handing over the name and address of that local witch, they should definitely be wary of this person.

"Yes," Cal agreed.

She looked at him. "You didn't like Varlan, did you? He made you nervous?"

Cal gave her a surprised look. "Of course he made me nervous. Were you in the same conversation I was? That seer is a killer. I don't know his story precisely, but he's clearly worked as an assassin… likely for centuries, given his age. I don't know how he got here, but I doubt it was the Light that sent him to us."

Alexis frowned.

Seeing it through Cal's eyes, she realized she agreed.

"About the only good thing about him is that he seemed to genuinely fear a repeat of what happened on his last world?" Cal muttered.

"What about your father?" she said, turning.

Cal's expression hardened perceptibly.

"What do you mean?"

"Do you think he is coming after us? Or will he be more focused on trying to re-open the portals first?"

Cal frowned. Then, slowly, he shook his head.

"I don't know for sure," he admitted. "I don't know enough to be certain. But if I had to guess, he's likely trying to contact these same beings, the 'Dark Gods.' He's probably casting spells as we speak… unless there's some reason he can't do it on a boat. He won't wait, if he can help it. Although…"

The White Dragon hesitated, as if not sure he should voice the rest out loud.

But Alexis suspected she knew what he'd cut himself off from saying.

"He's coming after me," she finished for him. "I know. It occurred to me that maybe he needs a Lightbringer to talk to these things. Varlan really seemed to make a point of mentioning that. Like he was warning us. Or warning me, at least."

Cal's jaw hardened again.

Then he shrugged.

"Varlan certainly likes his little games," he said, his voice carefully neutral. "From what I can tell, there wasn't much he said directly, if he could find a way to twist himself into a pretzel to hint about it, instead."

Alexis grunted, but not with a lot of humor.

Again, she agreed with Cal.

"Regardless," the Traveler said, exhaling. "If these 'Dark Gods' will only communicate with certain breeds of supernatural… or even *only* Lightbringers… it makes sense my father would want you close by. He might have even used my mother for a similar purpose while she was alive…"

His mouth firmed, and briefly, Alexis had to restrain herself from touching him.

The wound there was so deep, so tangible, it actually hurt her.

It felt like a hard knot of pain in the center of her chest.

Cal cleared his throat.

He shook his head, as if shaking off the memory of his mother.

"It's possibly he'll try to kidnap you," he added, his voice harder. "I half-expected that already, to be honest... he was so clearly focused on having you with him when we faced him on my world. I could tell, even then, that you were the important one to him. He would have run me through with a sword himself, without a second thought... but he wanted you alive. He was positively salivating about it."

Cal's voice grew openly bitter.

It held a colder fury when he went on.

"Now, at least, we have a better idea of why. He clearly thinks, at the very least, that having a Lightbringer nearby will strengthen his likelihood of success. Regardless of what he needs you for *exactly* within his rituals, he will likely try to move on us soon. We need to be ready. He will be desperate. My father, desperate, is not something you want to see."

Alexis nodded.

She didn't disagree with any of that, either.

It hit her again, how strange it was to have a partner in this, after so many years of working alone. It didn't feel like working with Devin or Jules, or any of the wolves in Devin's pack, or any of the vampires, witches, fallen angels, or demons she'd ever hired or worked with in Los Angeles or at any of her clubs.

This felt more...

Equal? Natural?

Permanent?

She couldn't decide, exactly.

Whatever it was, it unnerved her how totally comfortable she was with the idea of having him as her partner in such things.

She pushed the thought aside.

Right now, she needed to think.

"What if we did that?" she said. "I mean, we go to the sorceress Mara gave us, yes. But your father, he's already conjured these beings, right?"

"You mean wait for him to do it, then politely remind him that they only wish to speak to you?" Cal lifted an eyebrow. "Seems a bit risky, my love."

Alexis gave him a half-amused look.

She didn't disagree.

That also hadn't been the question she was asking.

She was pretty sure Cal knew that.

"I *do* know." Cal aimed a harder frown at her. "Pardon me for preferring the other thing you were thinking... about the two of us being partners. About how natural it feels between us. How right. How much I would like it to be permanent. How much I'm hoping it perhaps could involve some smaller versions of ourselves at some point..."

Exhaling at her incredulous stare, he threw up a hand.

"I agree with you, Lightbringer! I like it, too. I like it a lot. In fact, I like it so much, I have a full-blown hard-on right now, just from listening to you think about it. You've almost completely obliterated my ability to think about anything apart from sex..."

Her jaw dropped.

When she closed her mouth, about to retort an answer, he raised his hand.

His eyes and voice grew warning.

"I know what you were asking me, Alexis. I'll be honest... I don't have an answer yet. But if I had to give you one now, I'd say no. No, we should *not* try to force dear old Dad to give us the spell he uses to summon the Dark Gods. We shouldn't use my father to find or contact the Dark Gods at all. In fact, we should try to ensure he's *nowhere near us* when we make our own attempts to bargain with these creatures. Using my father in any way should be an *absolute last resort.* Which means, the sooner we do this, the better. I think it would be a disaster for us to wait until he reaches us here."

Alexis didn't answer.

Still, in turning over what he'd said, she frowned.

She agreed with him.

She almost didn't want to that time, but she did.

"So?" he said, his lips pinched. "What now, Lightbringer? Do we go back to the hotel? Get your friends? Or do we go to meet this sorceress on our own?"

Still thinking, he gazed out over the water, his voice taut.

"...Or do we skip this shady sorceress of Varlan's altogether? Use one of your own people? Is there anyone you trust who might serve us better in this? In your home city, perhaps?"

Alexis pursed her lips.

Truthfully, now she was having trouble not thinking about the other thing they'd been talking about. Pushing it from her mind, she exhaled in frustration.

She wished she had her damned portal magics.

Getting on a plane right now, for roughly fifteen to twenty-two hours, felt like a terrible idea. Really, when she thought about it now, after everything Varlan and Mara had said, it felt entirely out of the question. Even thinking about it made her nervous as hell.

Losing that much time to the Red Dragon, given everything she sensed happening, everything Mara and Varlan warned them about, sounded downright foolhardy.

She *did* have more faith in her Los Angeles contacts, of course.

She'd worked with them more.

She trusted them more.

In Los Angeles, Alexis knew powerful witches and warlocks.

She even knew a few vampires with some serious magical kick.

She had access to people with real gifts there.

Then there was Devin's girlfriend.

From what Devin had told her, Gabriela was a pretty damned powerful witch. She also happened to be one of the senior witches to a major Los Angeles coven. In this case, senior meaning "one of the most powerful," not "one of the oldest" of the group.

Possibly, via Devin, Alexis could get the entire coven to help her over the phone.

Possibly, it would be just as strong, just as effective, to do that kind of magic long distance as it would be to do it in person.

She could at least set them up as backup, maybe to aid the Thai sorceress on the ground here, the one whose name Mara gave her.

At least then they'd have someone magical watching their back.

She thought about Cal's other question.

But Alexis didn't want to go back to the hotel yet.

She didn't want to drag Devin and Jules into this, not until she had real, concrete news to give them. She didn't want to bring them to Mara's sorceress before Alexis herself had checked her out. She didn't want to endanger her friends at all, not without a damned good reason.

She wanted more information first.

Cal snorted. "Funny how you don't worry about me so much, Lightbringer."

She snorted back, nudging him with an elbow.

She didn't let herself think too clearly about what he'd said that time, either.

14

WHATCHAMA-WHOSIT

*I*n the end, she called them.

Well, she called the hotel suite.

Devin picked up the phone.

"Hey," she said. "It's me." She looked at Cal, then firmed her jaw. "We've just met with the seers. We're likely going to make one more stop. But we'll be back soon."

"'Lex—"

"Just listen, Dev."

She gave him a high-level summary of what the two seers said, including that Mara gave them the name and address of a local sorceress.

Alexis then told them to stay in the hotel.

She again advised them to get some sleep.

She told them to be ready to leave, hopefully in the morning.

Devin tried to hide it, but Alexis practically felt his relief at that last part.

The longer she talked, the more Alexis found herself glad she was doing this over the phone, and hadn't opted to go back to the hotel to deal with Devin or Jules in person.

Her two friends definitely would have tried to talk her into skipping the Thai sorceress and booking them flights back to LAX, asap.

As it was, Devin pointed out she'd gotten the referral from two deeply bizarre-sounding seers, only one of whom Alexis even *sort of* knew, and both of whom may or may not be evil themselves.

If Alexis had gone back to the hotel, Jules definitely would have chimed in on Devin's side. Both of her best pals would have tried to pressure her into going home, as in go home *right now,* to work with people they all knew and trusted in L.A.

Alexis could even see their point.

Based on what Mara and Varlan said, there was some chance the Red Dragon couldn't do his summoning spell without her. If she headed for Los Angeles now, that might be as good a way as any to put distance between her and Cal's jackass of a dad.

If the Red Dragon needed her nearby for his Dark Gods summoning spell, the world's only Lightbringer being on an airplane over the Pacific Ocean might be the most effective means of thwarting him in the short term.

But, as logical as it sounded when Devin said it, Alexis' gut screamed it would be a huge, terrible, world-ending mistake.

Alexis also knew Devin.

She knew full-well the werewolf's highly logical mind was mostly being employed simply to generate a highly logi-cal-sounding excuse.

Devin and Jules were *dying* to go home.

Alexis could hear it in Devin's voice, even now.

Devin was feeling the alpha werewolf thing, big time. It had definitely grown worse than when she'd last seen him, probably because he'd spent the last hour or so talking to every member of his pack, if only to reassure them all he was still in one piece.

Alexis had exactly zero doubt what the pack would be telling Devin to do.

Jules wasn't much better, truthfully.

The half-fae was one of the most social people Alexis knew, with friends all over Los Angeles, not to mention a large and tight-knit adoptive family of *very* outgoing humans who more or less worshipped the ground Jules walked on.

Devin told Alexis the phone had been ringing off the hook in the suite since she and Cal left to meet with the seers, and Alexis one hundred percent believed him.

Devin also mentioned Jules had gotten her new smart phone delivered, thanks to the Alexis' people at The White Rabbit, and that Jules having her own phone hadn't slowed down the calls coming in on the landline much at all.

Jules had already spoken to people at The Red Whip multiple times, first to tell them she and Alexis were alive... then to say they were on their way home... then to check on operations there... then to talk to several people who called the hotel just to hear her voice.

Jules also called her sister in Santa Monica, only to get screams, cries of joy, and tears through the phone.

Not surprisingly, her entire family had been completely freaking out the entire time she'd been gone; they'd been positive she and Devin were kidnapped and/or murdered.

Given how Devin's wolf pack found his house tossed, Jules' car in the driveway parked next to Devin's, his glass sliding door and kitchen windows shattered, the garage door with a big hole in it, signs of a fight on the front yard...

...not to mention the blood...

Everyone pretty much feared the worst.

They'd also immediately called the police.

The pack tried to track them, of course, but lost their scent at the Old Zoo… for pretty obvious reasons.

Devin snorted a laugh when he told her how crazy Jules' family had been over the past hour or so, but Alexis hadn't been sure how it was funny.

She still felt horrible she'd put her friends in danger.

She felt horrible she'd scared Jules' parents and siblings so badly.

As for the phone conversations, she'd overheard some of that herself, before she left the hotel suite with Cal.

She'd heard Diana, one of the waitresses at The Red Whip, squeal so loudly over the phone when she heard Jules' voice on the line, Jules pulled the hotel's phone receiver away from her ear with a laugh.

Jules told them all over dinner, her mouth half-full of Pad Thai, that she'd probably have to spend the next month taking people out to lunch and coffee to explain what happened to her, and that they'd better come up with a damned good story before then.

"…Preferably on the plane ride home," she'd said darkly, giving Alexis a meaningful stare as she emphasized the *going back home* part. "In fact, I think we should do that the whole way home *tomorrow*, 'Lex…"

Again, the hint hadn't been subtle.

Devin had grunted in agreement.

Sitting with them around the coffee table, Devin told them he'd called Vic, his second in the North Hollywood pack. According to Dev, the other werewolf about lost his mind, and actually started *shouting* at him before Devin could explain shit.

Devin also muttered that he'd called his girlfriend, Gabriela, and spent twenty minutes on the phone reassuring her after she burst into tears.

Alexis actually overheard part of that conversation—

unintentionally, of course.

When she'd come out of the shower in a terrycloth robe to find Devin in the bedroom with her, on her phone, she was pretty sure he'd been in the middle of that conversation.

Grabbing her new, mostly-empty carry-on bag, half-filled with clothes she'd bought at the Penang Airport, she'd retreated into the walk-in closet, closing the door most of the way behind her. While she hung her newly-bought clothes on the hotel's wooden hangars, hoping to get some of the wrinkles out, she couldn't help but overhear Devin speaking quietly into the phone in the other room.

She'd tried not to listen, especially not to details, but she knew it must be his girlfriend, just from his tone of voice. She heard him repeat that he was *totally fine* a number of times, that he was alive, in one piece, and that he'd tell her everything as soon as he was back in L.A.

So yeah, Alexis understood her friends' desperation to go home.

She wanted to go home, too.

She might not have a werewolf pack, or a significant other waiting for her there, like Devin did, or a wacky family who adored her, or a zillion friends, like Jules did... but she looked forward to returning to her house on the hill over Sunset. She looked forward to her morning run in the park, and her favorite coffee place, and the gym where she worked out and sparred with Devin's pack of werewolves.

She wanted to go to the club and hear her employees gossip about the guests.

She missed the other werewolves in Devin's pack, and the witches she was friends with, and even a few vampires she knew around town.

She missed her morning breakfast burrito and almond-milk cappuccino.

More than any of that, she wanted to hunt down those

damned smoke creatures, and find some way to neutralize the last of them. She had Devin's people looking for them already, but she would definitely feel better leading that little scouting party.

Thinking through all that made her uncomfortable, though.

She couldn't help but notice the contrast between her own priorities and those of Devin and Jules.

She had no one to call, really.

The managers at her clubs... sure.

She could call them. See how business was going. Offer them support.

But really, Jules handled most of that.

They'd rather talk to Jules.

The only people she definitely *would* have called, under different circumstances, were Devin and Jules, themselves.

But Devin and Jules were already with her.

That left no one, really.

Of course, she'd have more people to contact, if the other Lightbringers—

Cal turned, sharply. His eyes shone with an open warning.

Alexis felt her jaw tighten.

Still, she changed channels smoothly in her mind.

—hadn't all been killed, she thought, a touch louder.

Cal's expression relaxed, but not by much.

Alexis fought to ignore it.

With an effort, she turned her mind back to her previous train of thought.

The bottom line was, most days, Alexis didn't at all feel lonely, or like she should have more people in her life. Still, in thinking about what she'd left behind in Los Angeles, it struck her that her life might be a little empty there.

It might be a little work-obsessed.

Okay, it might be *almost entirely* work-obsessed.

She found herself remembering all the times Devin and Jules gently hinted the same, hinting at her need to develop more relationships there... to *have more fun,* as Devin and Jules put it... and to build a life for herself outside of work.

For the first time, maybe ever, Alexis wondered if they were right.

She wanted to go home.

She absolutely wanted to go home.

But she didn't *need* to go home, not the way Jules and Devin did.

Cal snorted.

Alexis turned to glare at him.

In the process, she stepped off the curb to get around another group of tourists. A horn blared behind her. Turning her head, she dodged a *tuk-tuk* by jumping back to the sidewalk, weaving through the bar and restaurant crowd.

They were on a larger street now, one that ran parallel to the river.

"Seers can do that, you know." Cal looked over at her, rejoining her side when they got past the crowd around the bar door. "...They can affect your mind. Just by being close to them. Close to their 'living light,' as they call it."

He gauged her face, his eyes a new-leaf green.

"I've heard such proximity with seers can cause... how did they phrase it? 'Unwanted bouts of tragic introspection.'"

Alexis blinked.

Then, when his words fully sank in...

She grunted an involuntary laugh.

"Unwanted bouts of tragic introspection?" she said.

Cal nodded with mock seriousness.

"The bastards exude a kind of meditative, introspective, whatchama-whosit field of one kind of another." He glanced at her with a wry smile. "...Or so I was led to understand. It puts you in some kind of 'spiritual space' that forces you to think about the meaning of your life, whatever elements your life may be missing, or lacking, or out of balance. Any causes of unconscious unhappiness or needed growth... and other irritating things."

She quirked an eyebrow at him. "Whatchama-whosit?"

Cal nodded, smiling a little. "Indeed. I believe that is the technical term."

Reaching over, he took her hand, squeezing her fingers in his.

"So we are staying then?" he said. "In Bangkok. To meet this sorceress?"

He lifted her hand to his lips, kissing her palm.

She shivered at the touch of his mouth, in spite of herself.

His voice deepened, turning back to the voice of a king.

"I admit, it wasn't easy to follow that particular labyrinthian tangle of your thoughts... but it seemed to be coming down on you and I meeting with that sorceress tonight, then deciding if we want to call in some of your witchy pals from your home town to assist in some sort of dark magic ritual or whathaveyou... or fly back to your city on that other continent."

She fought with how to react to his words.

There was the kiss.

There was that deeper voice.

Then there was that cavalier dismissal of her stream of consciousness. Some part of her wanted to be amused that he'd listened to all of that, even as another part of her felt annoyed, even strangely defensive.

Possibly even embarrassed.

She knew how easily he read her mind.

She'd almost gotten used to it.

But it still managed to make her feel like an idiot on occasion.

She cleared her throat.

"I think that is our next course of action, yes," she said stiffly. "I would like to go see that sorceress now. With you… and without the others. Then we can know if we are staying a few days more, or leaving tonight."

She gave him a sideways look.

He studied her face.

Then, as if in disbelief, he let out an exasperated sound.

"Gods and sandwiches! Are you really going to make me say it? You have a *life,* Lightbringer," he burst out, voicing that exasperation.

He now sounded genuinely unsure if he should be annoyed or amused.

"…Archangels above! You have enough 'life' to fill the banal realities of a dozen shifters, humans, and half-faelings. Not to mention seers with annoyingly long lives and even more annoying 'wisdom.' You simply are burdened with a horribly, maddeningly, intrinsically crucial and *important* job, Alexis. You know… that little thing you do, keeping an entire dimension safe from dark beings and malignant forces? Pretty much single-handedly?"

Alexis rolled her eyes at him.

They walked a few more steps.

Thinking about his words, she snorted.

That time, she also shook her head.

The Traveler was ridiculous.

Many, many beings kept the dimensions safe.

She was far from doing it alone.

Laughably far. Incalculably far. She was but one tiny game piece on an enormous board, one with too many moving parts for her to comprehend even a fraction of it.

Still, she did feel better.

A little better, maybe.

Cal squeezed her hand harder.

"Of course you do."

She looked over at him, quirking an eyebrow. "I'm not sure if I can blame the seers, though, Caliginous," she admitted with a small smile. "I was thinking a lot of those things before we went over there. I've been thinking them for months."

"Fuck seers," he said decisively. "Of *course* you can blame them."

A silence fell between them.

Of course, it was a silence *only* for the two of them, as it was punctuated with honking car horns, the higher beeps of *tuk-tuks*, mopeds, and motorcycles with loudly revving engines as they roared by. Drunken shouts and laughter rose from nearby bars as they passed, not to mention the sounds of breaking glass, thumping music, and yells of the vendors.

All of those noises grew louder as they drew even with the mouth of an alleyway filled with shop fronts, outdoor cafes, kiosks, touristy T-shirt shops, and booths selling elephant pants and skirts, along with scarves and tie-dyed sarongs in a rainbow of colors.

Alexis found herself turning over Cal's words.

Then, involuntarily...

She snorted a laugh.

15

A NEW DEVELOPMENT

*C*al helped. Strangely, his weird summary and dismissal of the seers helped a lot.

She managed to refocus on the problem at hand, starting with everything Mara and Varlan told them… and everything they didn't.

As she turned over their actual words, one by one, she realized just how many holes lived in the story they'd given her and Cal.

The two seers had been cryptic at best.

Really, Mara had said very little at all.

She'd barely spoken the whole time they'd been there, letting her far more unnerving mate do practically all of the talking.

And yet, according to Varlan, Mara was the expert. According to Varlan, Mara had to be the one to explain the nature of the Dark Gods, but Mara never really *had* explained it.

Well, not in a way that made a heck of a lot of sense.

She told them the Dark Gods were beings who lived in this dimension, and in many other dimensions, sometimes more or less simultaneously. She told them the Dark Gods rarely "picked sides" in terms of the life cycles or travails of other beings with whom they lived.

Then, minutes or seconds later, Mara also told them that the Dark Gods interfered occasionally, for reasons no one (apparently) really understood.

As to whether they were genuinely "Dark" or genuinely "Light" in nature, Mara didn't really have an answer for that, either. She seemed to think they lived somehow outside of that spectrum. Later, though, she said something off-hand about how they were *probably* dark.

Or, she amended, they *might* be dark.

Or not.

Or maybe they were dark only sometimes, or from a certain perspective.

She didn't really know.

Alexis had been half-ready to strangle the female seer by then.

In any case, the number of people who could actually summon one of the Dark Gods to speak to it appeared to be pretty small.

Even with the sorceress, Mara sounded vague.

She'd said she thought a local witch-doctor of sorts might be able to pull off a summons.

Or the sorceress might know someone who could.

Or she might know how they could get ahold of a spell book that would tell them how to do it, and what kinds of beings might be needed.

In the end, Alexis mostly tuned Mara out.

When Mara finished speaking, Alexis bowed, using the polite seer form.

Then she took the piece of paper with the sorceress' name and address written on it from Mara's fingers. She thanked Mara and Varlan—probably a little overly-brusquely

—even as she began backing towards the hallway leading to the front door.

Mostly, she just wanted to get the hell out of there without Cal punching one or both of them in the face.

By the end of Mara's explanation, she could practically *feel* the Traveler King's anger.

She could also feel Cal's restraint.

He'd stood behind her by then, clenching his hands periodically at something particularly vague or maddening said by Mara or Varlan or both of them. She suspected it took every ounce of his willpower to keep from snarling threats at the two seers.

Now she stared down at the piece of paper Mara had given her, and frowned.

The address they'd gotten was all the way across town, off Sukhumvit, one of the major arteries that cut through the middle of Bangkok.

"We should get a taxi," she said to Cal, still staring down at the numbers mixed with letters in the Thai language. "It will take too long on the Skytrain, and we're too far from the nearest station down here, anyway…"

She trailed when Cal touched her arm.

The Traveler came to a stop.

Alexis stopped with him.

Looking up, she found herself face-to-face with a strangely tall woman.

The woman before them had to stand at least six feet tall, and looked more like a seer than Mara did.

Whatever breed or species she was, this new female practically crackled with some kind of supernatural power, something so different from Alexis' own, Lightbringer power, she couldn't help but frown.

The woman's long, dark-blue hair hung past her shoulders, but the front part had been tied back in a half-ponytail,

and braided along the sides of her head. The style accentu-
ated already-high cheekbones, and an emaciated, skull-like
face.

Everything about the woman struck Alexis as bony,
angular.

Her teeth were strange, Alexis couldn't help noticing.

Her lower jaw held two strangely-long, canine-like teeth.

They stood up past her upper teeth, shaped almost like
upside-down fangs.

"You are Alexis Poole?" the woman said.

There was no threat in her words, or even any curiosity.

Alexis glanced at Cal.

He lifted an eyebrow in response, but she saw a wariness
in his eyes. She also felt his attention on the backpack she
wore—the one filled almost to the brim with weapons.

Alexis found herself doing a mental inventory of those
weapons now, starting with her whip, which should sit on
top, the two loaded Glocks with their extra magazines, and
the assortment of knives she'd brought, to go with her longer
hunting knife.

Alexis looked back at the woman with the dark blue hair.

"Yes," she said, blunt. "I am Alexis Poole. Who are you?"

The woman didn't so much as blink.

Alexis' borderline threatening tone clearly didn't faze her.

"I was sent," the woman said. "I am to bring you safely to
Narissa."

Alexis glanced down at the name written on the piece of
paper in her hand.

In Thai, it read: *Narissa Koh, 720 Sukhumvit 77, Wattana,
Bangkok.*

She showed the piece of paper to Cal, who frowned.

"You know I can't read any of that, right?" he murmured.
"Looks a bit like bird droppings on parchment to me, so I
have no idea why you're giving me that facial expression."

She laughed, unable to help it.

It's the sorceress's name, she thought at him. *Narissa.*

She watched him frown, understanding reaching his eyes. He turned to look over the tall, skeletal woman with the dark blue hair.

After a brief perusal, he shrugged, barely perceptible.

"Your call, Lightbringer."

She pursed her lips, looking back at the tall woman.

"All right," Alexis said. She put the paper in her pocket. "Lead the way."

16

CLEA

The woman with the blue hair didn't take them to the address on the piece of paper Mara had given them.

When Alexis noticed, she immediately grew alarmed.

"Where are we going?" she said.

They were in a car now.

Alexis looked back over their shoulder, gazing out the window at the onramp Alexis had expected them to take to reach the freeway.

"...This isn't the way to the address we were given. You should have gotten on the freeway back there. That part of Sukhumvit will take too long to get to on side streets."

She and Cal sat alone in the back of the old-fashioned Rolls Royce. The antique vehicle was cream-colored on the inside, a warm brown on the outside. The woman with the blue hair drove, but from the right side of the car, cruising up the left lane, like in England.

She didn't play the radio.

She didn't close the separating window between them, either.

She did offer them drinks out of the small refrigerator in the back.

Both Cal and Alexis declined.

Now, the woman with the blue hair seemed entirely unfazed by Alexis' question.

She didn't react at all to the clear aggression in Alexis' voice.

"Yes," she said simply. "Narissa is not at home. This is why I came to find you. She thought it better if I intercept you, before you could go all the way to her residence... where she is not. I am to take you to where she is currently."

"Which is where?" Cal said, wary.

The woman with the blue hair looked at him in the rearview mirror, but didn't answer.

But silence wasn't an acceptable response for Alexis.

"Where are you taking us, friend?" Alexis asked. "Tell us. Now. Or this ride is over."

That time, the threat in her voice was unambiguous.

The woman's eyes shifted in the mirror, looking at Alexis instead of Cal.

She still didn't blink, or change expression.

Her eyes remained strangely blank, emotionless.

"I am taking you to your own club, Alexis Poole. Your club here in Bangkok. The White Rabbit. Narissa will meet you there."

Alexis' anger turned into something closer to bewilderment.

The White Rabbit?

All this cloak and dagger just to take her to her own property?

"Then why not just call us? Tell us to meet you at the club?" Alexis said. "Why all of this weird, vaguely-threatening bullshit?"

"We did not have your telephone number."

Alexis' frown deepened.

She exchanged flat-out skeptical looks with Cal.

"You don't have our phone number? But you could find us on the street?" Pausing, Alexis added, "You could have asked any person at the club to call me on your behalf. Unless you were doing something sketchy as hell, they would have left me a message."

Again, the blue-haired woman appeared unmoved.

"Narissa told me you went to see Mara and her mate," she explained patiently. "We are familiar with them. It was not difficult to find you." Her eyes shifted to Cal. "There are not many of your kind here. You are... distinctive."

Alexis wondered what the hell that meant, too.

This woman was starting to really push her buttons.

"I suppose *calling* Mara was out of the question?" Cal muttered under his breath to Alexis. "Couldn't her mistress have asked one of those batty seers to pass along a message? Seems a bit more efficient... and less insane..."

He obviously hadn't meant it as a question for the tall woman, but the woman answered him anyway. Her voice remained just as emotionless and polite as before.

"She does not carry a phone with her, Most Respected and Venerable White Dragon," she said. "Nor does she use phones at all, really. When she wishes to speak with someone, she goes to them. It is simply her way. We realize it is eccentric."

There was a silence.

In it, the woman's eyes flickered up.

She once more stared at Cal in the rearview mirror.

Headlamps from the car behind them hit her eyes and face.

Alexis noted for the first time that the woman's irises were a strange color. While mostly a dark tint of gold-orange, which was strange enough, they also contained streaks of rust-red. Not quite like veins, or blood, but more like spike-like stripes, they threaded through the primary color of those too-round orbs, making them look distinctly animal-like.

The black of her pupils was also unusually small, especially for it being dark out.

Alexis didn't see them contract in the light of the headlamps, either.

There was something deeply strange about the combination of those odd eye characteristics, something that struck Alexis as almost familiar.

"Given the constraints I outlined," the woman continued. "Sending me to find you is actually the most *efficient* course," the woman added belatedly. "Due to the lack of a phone. And her knowledge of the whereabouts of your prior meeting."

Alexis and Cal exchanged looks.

Alexis noticed the woman still staring at Cal.

She felt her hackles start to rise.

She bit her lip, forcing her eyes off the other female.

Whoever and whatever the blue-haired woman with the weird eyes was, and whatever she wanted with them, she definitely appeared to be too interested in Cal. Alexis noted the interest and curiosity in her eyes, mixed with something else.

That "something else" remained elusive, too subtle for Alexis to identify, but she was beginning to think the blue-haired woman wanted him.

Not like that was unusual.

The sheer number of women staring at him in Old Town Bangkok already had her teeth on edge.

Cal chuckled, sliding closer to her. He stroked her hair back from her face, caressing her jaw. "You really are one to talk, my dear. Then again, I've noticed you are deeply oblivious to how many males and females stare at you when you walk down the street. I can't decide if it's maddening or adorable."

So she does want to sleep with you? Alexis asked in her mind, turning to look at him.

"No," Cal murmured softly, kissing the side of her face.

She is way too interested in you. She stares at you. Constantly. If it's not sex, then what is it? What does she want with you?

He took her hand, pulling it out of her lap and into his.

"Shifter," he muttered under his breath.

Alexis stiffened.

What?

"Shifter."

He leaned closer.

He spoke so low into her ear, his lips touched her skin, his words merging with the car's engine. She heard his meaning as much through the vibration as the actual sounds.

"Shifter," he repeated softly. "They always react to our kind strangely."

Alexis blinked.

This woman was a shifter?

Seriously?

What kind of shifter? She sure as hell wasn't a werewolf.

She looked up at Cal with a frown.

He nodded perceptibly, his eyes grim as they flickered towards the woman seated in front of them, gripping the ivory-colored steering wheel.

Before Alexis could think a coherent reaction to that, the woman spoke.

Obviously, she had a shifter's sense of hearing.

"Yes, I am a shifter." Her voice still entirely lacked any kind of inflection. "I apologize for not introducing myself earlier. My name is Clea. I am an elephant shifter."

"Elephant?" Alexis couldn't stop herself from expressing surprise.

Some part of her wanted to doubt the woman's assertion.

"Really? Elephant? I've never even heard of an elephant shifter before."

"We're not… common," the woman said.

She looked in the rearview mirror again.

That time, she met Alexis' gaze.

"I find it easier to be an elephant here," the woman confessed. "The risks are still great, wherever my kind live. But here… it is easier. Marginally."

Cal and Alexis exchanged another look.

Then Cal looked at the blue-haired woman's eyes in the rearview mirror.

"I can imagine that," he said politely.

The woman didn't answer.

She also didn't elaborate further.

17

DAHLIA

*I*t was strange as hell to be back in one of her own clubs, even if it was in Bangkok, instead of her flagship location on Sunset Boulevard.

It was odder still to be led inside by a perfect stranger, and told she would be brought to one of the private booths in the back, to meet with Narissa Koh.

No one in the club's lobby recognized her.

Then again, she wasn't exactly dressed the way she normally did when she surveyed one of her properties— much less when she made a show of playing hostess as the owner.

She could have made an issue of it, of course.

She could have announced who she was, demanded the A-List treatment due to her as the owner and sole proprietor.

She chose not to do that.

She kept an office in every property she owned, so she'd have a place to work whenever she came to visit. She hadn't been to this particular club in quite some time, but she knew her people would have kept her office pristine, likely cleaning it every other day and making sure her fish got fed and her plants watered.

She liked having living things in her offices.

The two girls working the front were young, Thai, and looked and acted relatively new. Alexis didn't micro-manage her properties, but she traveled enough to have a passing familiarity with anyone who had worked in one of her properties for more than a few months.

These two clearly had no idea who she was.

They'd likely heard her name spoken by the more seasoned staff, and possibly had even seen photos of her around the club, or even in magazines. Even so, it struck Alexis as much less likely they would recognize her in person. Most of those photos were touched up, or simply lit to perfection, and all of Alexis' smiles and angles were posed.

Moreover, whenever she attended a gala or other event, Alexis was heavily made up and dressed to the nines. Even if these two hostesses were huge fans, Alexis had her doubts they would have recognized her, given how she looked now.

Alexis didn't have a lot of candid photos of her show up in the Hollywood news.

She tended to avoid having her likeness passed around.

The fewer people who knew her by sight, the better.

She very much preferred remaining behind the scenes, and not only because a high profile potentially put everyone she knew and cared about at risk.

The last thing she needed were some Hollywood slacker kids seeing her hack up demons in Griffith Park, recognize her, tell everyone they knew, and post it on social media with her name attached and "OMG!!!" in the caption.

For the same reason, she wasn't the slightest bit offended they didn't know her at the front lobby of The White Rabbit.

If she'd been alone, she might have been *forced* to tell them who she was, if only because of her clothes. They might not have let her in otherwise; technically The White Rabbit had a dress-code.

But because she and Cal walked in with the blue-haired elephant shifter, Clea, as guests to "Mistress Narissa," who clearly had some kind of favored-client status with The White Rabbit staff, the hostesses were all smiles.

The obviously senior staffer of the two working the front desk walked round the podium and clasped Clea's hand. She aimed smiles at Alexis and Cal only after she'd greeted the tall woman with the strange eyes, those odd tusks, and the skeletal face.

If the hostess had a disapproving look or thought for Alexis in her too-casual clothing, which included a backpack full of weapons and lace-up combat boots, she kept it to herself.

Instead the woman bowed deeply to all three of them.

Then, still smiling, she turned to lead them deeper into the dark-walled club.

It wasn't until they reached the main floor that Alexis heard a surprised squeal and turned, realizing she'd been recognized after all.

"Lex!"

A voice thick with a Brooklyn accent called out her name from across the bar.

As Alexis turned, a woman with long, brown curls leapt up from a leather barstool, landing lightly on the heels of leather shoes that had to be six inches high.

She practically ran over the club's slick floor in those teeteringly high heels.

Despite what looked like a painfully tight dress, her face was all smiles. She reached where 'Lex, Cal, Clea, and the hostess stood, and enveloped Alexis in a warm hug.

By then, Alexis had even remembered her name.

She was one of the dancers.

She used to work at the New York club.

She must have asked to transfer here.

"Oh, my dearest! I'm SO HAPPY TO SEE you!"

She squeezed Alexis tighter, then let go, beaming into her face.

"Jules called, of course," the woman said. "But I'm SO GLAD you came down here to prove to us you're alive and well! We all heard EVERYTHING when Jules and Dev vanished in Los Angeles! Rumors swirled that you might be somewhere in Asia, but when you didn't show up, people thought something might have happened to all THREE of you! OH MY GOD, it was like a HORROR movie!"

Taking a breath, she squealed, beaming at Alexis again, shaking her in her hands.

"OH MY GOD, YAY! I'm SO GLAD everyone was wrong! I'm so glad you are all okay! WHEN did you get here? Are you going to stay in Bangkok for a while, all three of you? We HAVE to go out! There are SO MANY FUN THINGS to do here!"

The woman spoke so quickly and loudly, in such a high voice, Alexis felt like she was getting repeatedly hit in the face.

She fought to get her equilibrium back, returning the woman's smile a bit blankly, staring into her heavily made-up face, which was only a few inches from hers. The woman's irises and pupils flickered in the dim light of the room, as if fighting to see her better.

They struggled to see accurately through the dark, colored contact lenses she wore.

It was a reminder of what she was.

"Vampire," Cal murmured from next to her. "You do keep the most interesting company, Lightbringer."

The vampire's eyes shifted to him.

She blinked, did a double-take.

Then she looked him over predatorily with her vampire eyes.

"My, my, my," the vampire murmured. "What have we here?"

Once she'd given him a thorough head-to-toe, more or less undressing him with her eyes, the vampire's lips rose in a delighted grin.

"And who is this scrumptious little snack you have with you, Mistress 'Lex?" The vampire never took her eyes off Cal's face. "Damn. I bet he's even prettier without his clothes. Wherever did you find him? And is whatever he's got between his legs the real reason you went 'missing'? Because oh my GOD that is a story I want to hear…"

She looked at Alexis, seemingly oblivious to the fact that her boss had tensed, losing her smile more and more, the longer the vampire gawked at the Traveler.

"Damn," the female vamp repeated. "I have to admit, I'm dying to ride this one myself." Her crystal eyes flashed under the dark contact lenses. "Maybe just a little taste, too… if he's not the squeamish type…"

Alexis felt her jaw harden to stone.

The vampire didn't seem to notice that, either.

"…If you're open to sharesies," the vampire offered. "I'd absolutely *kill* to use him in the floor show later tonight." The vampire continued to look the Traveler King over, now with a measured look, her hands on her hips as she stared at his crotch. "The crowd would absolutely *adore* him. Especially with that adorable little snarl he's giving me right now…"

The vamp winked at Cal, whose eyes went cold.

When she ran a light hand over his jaw, Cal jerked his face away, without moving back, but with a real glare.

"Don't touch," he snapped.

The vampire's lips slid into another delighted grin.

"Fuck. This one is sex on a stick. I'm positively *dying* to see him strapped down and…" She ran her tongue over a slightly-extended fang. "…Attentive."

"Down, Dahlia," Alexis said.

She kept her voice light, but even she heard the edge there.

"This one isn't for playing with," she added, just as tautly.

Cal looked at her, then stared back at the vampire, who pushed out her lower lip in a pout.

"Greedy, greedy," the vamp murmured. "Are you sure I can't talk you into it, Mistress? I'll treat him ever so nice. I'll be on my best behavior—"

"I'm sure," Alexis said, colder. "He's not a toy, Dahlia."

"Are the two of you—"

But Alexis cut her off.

"Dahlia, no." Her voice grew openly warning. "Don't ask again. And don't touch him again, either. He's already asked you once." Pausing, she added more meaningfully, "You're being rude, Dahlia."

Sighing, the vampire tore her eyes off Cal reluctantly.

She focused on Alexis with a small sigh.

Her posture went totally submissive.

"Fine," she said, her voice pouting. "What can I help you with, Mistress?"

Alexis, who'd been thoroughly distracted by the female vampire practically molesting Cal right in front of her, remembered why they were there. She glanced to her right, where Clea stood with the hostess from the front of the club.

They'd given the threesome some space, but were clearly waiting for them.

Looking back at Dahlia, Alexis rested her hands on her hips.

"I'm here to meet someone." When the vampire opened her mouth to speak, Alexis held up a hand. "We don't need an escort. Just keep an eye on security out here for us. And call

Jules. Let her know we're here, and that we're meeting with the person I told her about."

Dahlia's eyes followed Alexis' to Clea.

Alexis saw understanding flood the vampire's expressive face.

"Narissa?" she said. "You're here to see Narissa? Why, 'Lex?"

Alexis frowned.

She wasn't in the habit of explaining herself to employees.

Friends, sure, but Dahlia wasn't a friend.

She was significantly less likely to ever be a friend, after this little display. Even beyond Cal being hers, Alexis didn't like it when people treated others so disrespectfully. She didn't like it when people treated total strangers as if they were objects for their amusement.

Cal's hand closed on her waist.

He stepped forward, murmuring densely in her ear.

"Yours?" he purred softly. "Did I hear that correctly... Mistress?"

A fierceness lived in his words, a heat that made her tense.

She shivered, but didn't look back.

He continued to grip her waist.

"Damn, that is *hot*," Dahlia said.

Cal and Alexis both glared at her, and she held up an apologetic hand.

"Sorry! I'm sorry! Just an observation," she said meekly.

Alexis sighed internally. She wasn't crazy about Dahlia, she decided. Even for a vampire, she was kind of skewing sociopathic in Alexis' mind.

At the same time, she wasn't adverse to a little more information.

"What do you know about her?" she said, jerking her chin

lightly towards the elephant shifter. "This Narissa? We have only met her employee so far."

Clea didn't react to their stares or gestures.

She stood maybe twenty feet away from them now, waiting stoically by the entrance to a hallway that would take them to the club's private rooms. Most of those rooms consisted of soundproof "play areas" for guests, but a few more conventional, less sex-oriented spaces also resided in the far back. Those contained leather booths, wall monitors, sometimes dancing poles and wet bars, with polished wood tables and their own waitstaff for private meetings.

One even had a full conference table.

A few had private bathrooms.

Dahlia sighed, folding her arms.

Then, thinking about Alexis' question, she gave an exaggerated shrug.

"She is a witch," Dahlia said, matter of fact. "But I'm sure you knew that part, already. They mostly call them sorceresses here... in Thailand, I mean. Something to do with the kind of magic they employ, which has to do with the land here... I think. But from everything I know, she's a witch, if with slightly different powers."

Alexis nodded, her lips pursed.

"Powerful?" she said.

Dahlia gave a nod. Her voice and expression grew more serious. "From what I've heard, yes. Very. Uniquely so. We've only hired her here for others... VIP types who have need of a witch with a reputation for getting results. But her reputation is pretty impeccable."

Alexis nodded.

None of what Dahlia said exactly reassured her, but it didn't send up any red flags, either.

"All right." Alexis glanced at Cal, then back at the leggy

vamp. "Keep an eye out, will you? And call Jules. Otherwise, we don't wish to be disturbed."

"Righty-O, boss," the vamp said cheerily.

She gave Cal another too-long look, her fangs extended, and Alexis definitely didn't like that, either.

Still, she decided it wasn't worth getting into it now.

Instead, she looked at Cal, tilting her head in the direction of the private rooms.

"Shall we?"

The sooner they dealt with this, the better.

"I agree," Cal murmured.

Letting go of her waist, seemingly reluctantly, he aimed a dark, verging-on-hostile look at the female vampire as she walked away. He watched her for a full beat, almost like he wanted to say something, but he didn't speak the whole time she sashayed back towards the bar in her tight dress. For a second, Alexis thought he might say something to her, meaning Alexis herself, then he seemed to change his mind.

Firming his mouth, he nudged Alexis' arm instead.

"Okay," he murmured. "Let us get this done."

Without another word, he turned on his heel and began crossing the dark-tile floor over to where Clea stood.

Hiking the backpack full of weapons higher on her shoulder, Alexis followed.

18

NARISSA

*A*lexis entered the back room warily.

She had to walk past Clea to do so, who stood by the door.

The human hostess who led them here had already receded into the background, presumably on Clea's request, bowing as she disappeared back down the dark corridor.

Inside the oddly-shaped room, the tables, counters, and open shelves were covered with lit candles, all of them white.

Alexis glanced around at all of the open flames, considered making a crack about fire hazards in her club, then didn't, looking instead for the other occupant of the room.

The private lounge was set up slightly differently than Alexis remembered, making her wonder if the witch had rented out the space more long-term, and thus changed the inside décor to align more closely with her tastes and requirements.

Some things remained that Alexis remembered.

A dark brown, sectional leather couch Alexis remembered picking out still filled most of the far corner of the room, with a low, traditional-style Thai table below, adorned with a hand-painted tea set. A stone fountain filled most of a built-out shelf on the wall, a few feet away from the couch. Water ran down over the black rocks while she watched, making a pleasant, lulling sound that mixed with the thick smell of incense in the space.

Alexis had picked out the fountains, too.

A white rug lay on most of the center of the floor, and Alexis remembered that.

A woman sat on that rug now, with a second low table before her, surrounded by cushions Alexis did not remember.

She didn't remember this particular table, either.

The heavy-looking square slab top appeared to be made of some white stone, and had carvings all along it, most of them similar to what Alexis had seen on Buddhist *wats* around Thailand, but also some that appeared more esoteric. She found herself wondering if some of the more unusual ones were even human.

If they were, they must have come from a somewhat less common or obscure culture or time period.

Alexis was betting the symbols were non-human, though.

Scattered bird feathers covered the top of the white stone surface, along with carvings in darker rock, and pieces of quartz, jade, amethyst, and a handful of other minerals, rocks, and semi-precious stones. A large, vertical, free-standing crystal stood to the left of the witch's elbow on a red coral stand carved in the shape of a dragon.

Alexis wasn't familiar with whatever type of crystal it was.

She didn't think she'd ever seen that exact pattern of colors before.

In the candlelight, it looked to be a pale yellow, with purple, or possibly dark red highlights in the center. Those highlights appeared to be glowing, but it may have been a trick of the light, or some reflection from all of those artistically-placed candles.

Alexis felt eyes on her, studying her, and turned to face the witch.

The woman appeared to be Thai.

She might have been Chinese.

She sat cross-legged on a large, black cushion, her back perfectly straight. She watched Alexis survey the room, her expression unmoving, and unapologetic.

When Alexis looked at her directly, however, the woman's eyes shifted.

They focused past her, on Clea by the door.

"You may leave us, my friend," she said gently.

Her voice was low, musical.

Alexis looked back to the elephant-shifter, and saw the tall woman nod, once, even as she caught hold of the door's handle and began to walk it closed.

The door shut with a soft click, and Cal and Alexis looked back at the witch who sat cross-legged behind the white stone table.

"You can sit," the woman said, as if Alexis had come to visit her club, rather than the reverse. "I've asked the hostess to bring us tea. Let me know if you'd like something else."

Her English contained no trace of an Asian accent.

She could have been from Los Angeles.

"Canada, actually," the witch said. "Vancouver. I've lived in Bangkok for about twelve years now. But I grew up in British Columbia."

Cal spoke before Alexis could.

"Well, you've certainly made yourself at home within my wife's property," he said, his voice a touch cold. "Were you about to offer to give her a tour, as well?"

Alexis had to hide a smile.

The witch didn't seem to take offense.

She smiled up at them, then again motioned them towards the cushions on the floor.

"Please, sit," she said, her voice more carefully polite. "I really didn't mean to be rude. And it wasn't some kind of passive-aggressive power play, I promise you. I just knew you and your wife had only recently returned to this dimension. I thought perhaps you both might prefer to be in the role of *guest* rather than have the burden of playing host."

"We don't have time to be either," Alexis said, her voice a touch hard. "We came here for a reason. We wish to hire you for a particular task—"

"I know why you are here," the witch said.

That time, a faint warning lived in her words.

She looked at Cal, then back at Alexis.

"Well?" she said. "Shall we begin?"

Cal and Alexis exchanged frowns.

The Traveler King didn't speak, but she swore she could almost hear his thoughts that time, just as he undoubtedly heard hers.

Neither of them trusted her.

Neither of them trusted any of this.

"I understand," the witch said calmly. "But, as you will no doubt realize, you don't have much choice but to use me, if you plan to conduct this ritual in Bangkok. If that's not good enough for you... of course I will understand."

She said the last with a lightness that struck Alexis as feigned.

Alexis frowned.

Instead of agreeing with the witch, she found herself wondering if that was true.

Were there really no other witches... or sorceresses... in Thailand as powerful as this Narissa? Generally, older witches had more magical punch, but Narissa looked to be less than thirty. Could she really be the most powerful witch in all of Bangkok?

"No," Cal said, giving her a sideways look. "It's not true."

Unlike before, he didn't try to hide his words from the witch. He'd likely decided it was futile, since she seemed to be able to read the minds of both of them.

"…But it *is* the more expedient choice," he added reluctantly.

He met Alexis' gaze when she looked over.

For a few seconds, they only looked at one another.

Then, almost as one, they nodded, and approached the carved stone table.

THE LAST LIGHTBRINGER

*T*hey sat next to one another, cross-legged, like the witch.

They sat side by side and close together, their knees touching.

Both of them occupied the opposite edge of the square table as where Narissa sat. Rather than spreading out over more than one side, they'd opted to sit together. Both of them studied the witch, even as Cal laid a hand on Alexis' thigh, a gesture that felt both protective and strangely like he felt compelled to touch her, perhaps to reassure himself.

Alexis strongly got the impression the witch missed none of this.

Now Narissa studied them both openly with dark eyes, as if taking an inventory of sorts.

"Can you do it?" Cal asked, blunt. "Can you summon the Dark Gods?"

"And can they open the portals?" Alexis threw in.

The witch just stared at them for a beat.

Then her eyes swiveled to the door as it opened, letting in a dim light from the hallway. Alexis and Cal turned their heads, right as the hostess from the front lobby walked in, bowing, a tray with a tea pot and three tea cups in the center.

The woman brought the tray over to the stone table, and set it on the table to the right of the witch. Without saying a word, the hostess poured out three cups, handing one to each of them with a bow.

Then, bowing a final time, she backed out of the room.

She closed the door behind her.

Alexis glanced down at her tea.

She didn't really like tea all that much, but if the witch needed her polite little games, Alexis could play along.

The witch smiled shrewdly.

"You can speak aloud, you know. I hear equally well, either way."

Cal let out an annoyed sound.

Alexis only shrugged.

"I'm aware of that," the Lightbringer said. "I thought thinking it might be faster. Many people who like playing games enjoy verbal sparring, and might prolong it for their own amusement."

Pausing to let that sink in, she added,

"I've found those same people are far less fond of having people think disparaging or condescending thoughts about them... and might choose to hurry things along."

"Or possibly sabotage your goals," the witch pointed out with a smile.

"Doubtful." Alexis peered at the witch over the top of her tea cup. "Your ego wouldn't permit my thinking you were incompetent... or less powerful than you wanted us to believe."

Cal let out a low snort.

The witch's smile widened.

"You really are quite clever, you know," Narissa remarked.

Alexis rolled her eyes.

Finishing her sip of tea, she lowered the cup to the table.

"Or quite stupid," she muttered under her breath. "I knew all this, yet allowed you to draw me into the verbal sparring match you wanted, anyway."

The witch laughed.

"You really are," the witch said, still smiling. "Clever. Particularly for a Lightbringer."

That time, Cal let out a low annoyed sound, almost a growl.

"I meant no offense." The witch glanced at him, then back at Alexis. "Most of your kind have always struck me as more hired muscle than strategists. I always assumed that was the way it was meant to be… the way you were genetically designed. It seemed your makers desired you to be biologically programmed in a way that kept you more or less one-minded in purpose, untiring in determination. Simple. Trainable. Deadly."

Lifting her own cup of tea, the witch shrugged.

"I suppose that is good luck for some of us, that I was wrong in my supposition. Bad luck for The Others, of course… and kind of ironic from a more universal perspective. That *you,* of all the Lightbringers the creators made, ended up being the guardian here, and the last Lightbringer in all the worlds. It is a strange sort of joke the Ancients might play. To choose you as the *only* Lightbringer… the last one standing after The Others killed the rest."

Alexis frowned.

Part of her wanted to pursue a few things in that little speech.

She had questions.

At the same time, she knew her own ego, and her own selfish interest in her Lightbringer origins, couldn't interfere with their purpose in being here.

She would leave her personal questions for later.

Right now, she had to figure out how to get what they needed out of the witch.

"Oh, I will do it for you," Narissa said, winking at her. "I was only yanking your tail a bit, Lightbringer. I like to know who I'm doing favors for..."

Cal let out another low growl, but the witch only gave him a sideways smile.

"...Particularly if those favors might cost me my soul."

And with that, with no preamble whatsoever...

Every candle in the room snuffed out.

THE SUMMONING

*C*al's hand tightened on her leg.

She didn't feel fear on him—mostly aggression, and a wave of protectiveness that affected her enough to surprise her.

As for Alexis herself, she went totally still.

It was the same thing that happened to her when she was hunting, or expecting an imminent attack.

She was still sitting there, breathing shallowly, otherwise unmoving, when a light bloomed into existence.

Dark, blood-purple and pale yellow, the illumination seemed to come from the ceiling itself at first. It pooled like liquid flame across the cream-colored paint, rippling in higher waves, flashing with veins of black and orange.

Cal nudged her, pointing to the table, and Alexis followed his nudge.

She focused on a dense thread of light connecting that pool of flame on the ceiling to the large crystal on one edge of the table. The thinner, denser strands seemed to come from the center of that crystal, and it struck Alexis that they were the same color.

After a few seconds of staring, she couldn't decide if the crystal anchored the light to the room, or if the light emanated from the center of the crystal, shooting up to create those strange, watery patterns on the curved surface overhead.

Wherever it came from, the light didn't really look like "light" at all.

It looked like gold and purple fire, like roiling flames.

It had a substance to it, something not quite smoke or water, but not quite light, either.

It really did look like fire—an otherworldly, magical fire.

Alexis found she couldn't look away from it, or the patterns it made on the ceiling.

The witch made a humorous sound. "It's a portal, Lightbringer. Of sorts. It is little wonder you are drawn to it, Alexis Poole."

Alexis tore her eyes off the ceiling, just long enough to look at the witch.

Narissa looked as otherworldly as the gold and purple flames.

Her face appeared to be mostly dark, except for her eyes, which burned with the same yellow flames as the ceiling overhead.

It struck Alexis that the color wasn't the usual yellow of fire.

There was something grittier about it, something strangely dark.

Not quite the color of urine, it wasn't the color of sunlight, either.

It spoke of death, of baked sand in the desert, of bleached bones.

"Are they there?" Alexis asked.

She found herself raising her voice, nearly shouting.

"Are the Dark Gods here?" she said, louder. "Have you

summoned them? Can we speak to them yet about the portals?"

"Only you can summon them, Lightbringer. I can only open the passage. I am the telephone, so to speak… you must be the voice."

Unlike Alexis, the witch spoke quietly, her voice low, deep, crystal clear in Alexis' mind, yet somehow a bare murmur.

Every word the witch spoke hit her like a blow to the face.

"I opened the portal," Narissa went on softly. "I can hold it open long enough for you to reach out… to make contact. But it must be *you* who speaks to them. It must be you who calls to them. You must do it now…"

The witch's eyes shifted to Cal.

She stared at him, and her voice grew a shade colder.

"…Only you. It can be *only you,* Lightbringer. No one else."

Alexis frowned, looking at Cal, then back at the witch.

What was it with everyone making a big deal about that?

The Red Dragon, Varlan… now this witch.

After the faintest hesitation, Alexis brushed off whatever misgiving or weirdness she felt around this whole thing. She tried to ignore the weirdness she felt between Cal and the other female, as well. Clearly Cal didn't like her. Just as clearly, Narissa felt the same about him. For Alexis' own part, she was already one hundred percent sure Narissa wasn't to be trusted, but maybe they didn't need to trust her.

They just needed her to do her part.

They needed her to open the door to the Dark Gods.

Which she claimed to have done.

Now Alexis just needed to figure out what to say to them.

Then they would pay her, and that would be the end of it.

"We are in total agreement on that, my love," Cal half-shouted.

Do you know her? Alexis asked in her mind. *The witch. It seems almost like you know one another somehow...*

Cal frowned, but he didn't answer her.

The witch didn't give him so much as a glance.

"Call to them!" she commanded to Alexis. "Call to the Dark Gods!"

Alexis meant to do just that.

Somehow, she hesitated again.

Somehow, a big part of her didn't want to.

Whether it was the gleam in the witch's eye, the shade of gold coming from the erect stone that wasn't really the gold of the Ancients she so loved... much less the pale blue she associated with her own, personal connection there... whether it was something in the witch's eagerness, or Cal's dislike, the words Narissa used, or some other, less tangible voice inside Alexis' mind...

Whatever the reason, she found she didn't want to.

She didn't want to do what the witch said.

Cal looked at her.

His mouth pursed.

He didn't look angry. He more looked puzzled.

She thought he would tell her to do it, to get this over with. She thought he would ask why she was prolonging things, when they both wanted to get the hell out of there.

He didn't, though.

He studied her face, his expression taut, like he was trying to feel whatever she felt... or perhaps trying to understand whatever he felt on her.

The witch's voice rose with the whirling lights.

"Call to them!" she cried out. "You must do it now! I know I said I would hold it for you, but I cannot keep the doors open forever, Lightbringer! You must call to them!

You must call to them NOW! Summon the Dark Gods NOW!"

"No," Alexis said.

She said it quietly, almost a whisper.

She didn't look at the witch as she said it.

She shook her head, staring at the light coming off the stone.

"No," she repeated.

This was wrong.

Everything about this was wrong.

"*What* is wrong?" The witch's voice hardened. "This is why you came to me, is it not? Why did you ask me to open this portal… at great risk to myself, I might add… if you had no intention of using it? Is this a trick of some kind? What is it you are waiting for, Lightbringer? Do you expect the Dark Gods to offer you a personal invitation?"

Alexis didn't answer.

Staring into the light, she frowned.

The witch's words pulled at her.

She could feel them trying to make her doubt herself.

If anything, that pull only hardened her resolve.

At the same time, she didn't have a *logical* reason for refusing, and she knew it.

What was her problem?

This was why they were here. They'd come to the witch for this exact thing.

Why was Alexis suddenly getting cold feet? Why the sudden doubt? Was it The Others working on her mind? Tricking her? Was the Red Dragon somehow in her head again?

"No," Cal said.

Alexis looked up, and he shook his head, adamant.

"No," he repeated. "I don't think so. That's not it."

"Then what is it?" she said, shouting with him.

"I don't know. But I would trust yourself over her."

He nodded towards the witch.

The witch raised her voice to match theirs.

"What is the problem?" she snapped. "Should I close the portal? Did you change your minds, Lightbringer, on re-opening the worlds? On bringing back the Light of the Ancients?"

Alexis frowned.

Had she? Was that what this was?

"I can't do it," she muttered, shaking her head. "I just can't. I can't."

"That's fine." Cal gripped her hand, holding it tightly on his thigh. "It's fine, 'Lex."

Something about him using her first name brought a pain to her heart.

A flood of emotion rose in her, so intense, it almost brought tears to her eyes. She looked down at their hands gripping one another, and it hit her that she loved him.

She really loved him.

She loved him so much it hurt.

She didn't know how that had happened, or even when, or why.

But it felt undeniably true.

It felt so true, she couldn't breathe.

"Alexis—" he began.

His voice came out rough, but she heard the emotion behind it. He looked about to say more, but before he could—

"WHAT?" the witch shouted. "WHAT did you say, Light-bringer?"

Cal turned on her.

The magic that lived in him, his Traveler magic, what he seemed to breathe out of his very skin, especially since they'd come back with her to this dimension, pulsed off him in a rippling cloud. It warmed her fingers, warmed her heart where it seemed to envelope hers, heated her throat and chest and even her face.

She felt his anger, a rush of protectiveness for her, an intensity of need to attack anything he saw as a threat to her person... and while normally she would have hated that kind of thing, this time it didn't scare her, or make her suspect he might be unhinged.

It didn't even annoy her.

She relaxed into it instead, even as it ignited the same feelings in her.

She felt one thousand percent on Cal's side.

Whatever he was fighting, whatever angered him... she would fight it, too.

Whoever his enemies were, they were her enemies, too.

He glared at the witch, his violet eyes turning to a pale, translucent blue.

"SHE SAID NO," Cal growled, half leaning over the table. "SHE SAID SHE WON'T *FUCKING DO IT.* SHE WON'T CALL TO THEM... SHE WON'T SUMMON THEM FOR YOU. NOW *BACK OFF,* OR I'LL KILL YOU MYSELF..."

Hostility and rage vibrated the Traveler King's voice.

It wasn't just distrust Alexis heard in his words.

It wasn't only fear, or anger.

It wasn't even *mostly* those things.

An overt animosity lived in his words, rippling off his skin.

Whatever it was, whatever it stemmed from, the sentiment struck her as personal. Something in the Canadian witch really rubbed Cal the wrong way. Like, in a visceral, quasi-*biological* way of rubbing someone the wrong way.

"You're not wrong, my love," Cal murmured.

Alexis frowned.

That hostility and anger still practically emanated from

Cal's skin, even as he wrapped himself around her, pulling her into his magic. In addition to loving him, she realized she trusted his instincts by now, too, even apart from that, which made her like the witch significantly, violently *less* than she already had.

With Cal, it was more than that.

Despite her empathetic reaction to the witch on his behalf, she could feel it was still nowhere near the negative reaction felt by the Traveler King himself.

Something about his reaction to her felt old.

Cal stared at the witch, frowning, almost like—

"Like you recognize her," Alexis muttered. "You do know her. You *know* her Cal. I don't know how, but somehow."

Cal turned, staring at Alexis.

She met his gaze. "You *know* her somehow, Cal. I can feel the part of you that is certain of it… but you can't remember where you met. Like she's…"

Alexis hesitated, even as a dawning understanding came over her.

The realization made her sick.

It made her sick because it felt utterly true.

"…Like she's *family*," Alexis finished.

Hearing herself say it out loud, she was suddenly, horribly certain she was right.

"Like she's *family*, Cal. Like she's *your* family…"

Cal stared into her face, into her eyes, frowning.

Then, suddenly, her words penetrated in a way that was real.

Understanding bloomed there, widening his pupils abruptly.

He turned, staring at the witch.

He stared at the glowing green face of the woman on the other side of the table for scarcely a beat of his heart before rising violently to his feet.

He shoved himself back from the table, still gripping Alexis' hand, pulling her with him. He stumbled backwards in obvious alarm, his arms out, his empty fist clenched, as if preparing to fight.

"ALEXIS!" he snarled. "GET BEHIND ME. NOW!"

She obeyed his words, more in instinct than conscious thought.

Leaping back from the table somewhat more easily than he had, she slid behind him, still gripping his hand as she stared past him at the witch. She kept inching forward until she once more stood by his side, only to be gripped more tightly by Caliginous' hand and pulled protectively closer to him.

She opened her mouth, about to ask…

…when a shocking flash of brilliance nearly blinded her.

Everything around them whited out.

THE ILLUSION

*A*lexis stumbled backwards a few steps more, urged by Cal's hand, which had released her fingers and now gripped her arm.

It wasn't only Cal that pulled her back.

She got shoved back too, by the violence of the silvery-white light.

Lightning-like sparks seemed to explode off the witch and the erect stone.

Alexis ducked them in reflex, even as the witch's voice rose from where she still sat, cross-legged, behind the table.

"SUMMON THEM!" the witch shouted. "SUMMON THEM, LIGHTBRINGER! WE MUST RE-OPEN THE GATES!"

Alexis stared at her, feeling a kind of horror rise in her gut.

Whatever that thing was, it wasn't human.

"It's my father," Cal shouted. "It is his energy, his magic… it is all the Red Dragon."

Cal spoke loudly from behind her, practically in her ear.

He half-shouted over the sound of wind rushing around them both.

Alexis' mind went to the cave, to the storm they'd encountered on the Traveler World, the one The Others had unleashed around that pyramid and the primary portal.

This storm felt like that one, Alexis realized.

It felt like the exact same storm had now been set loose inside the private back room of The White Rabbit.

"I don't know how it took me so long to recognize it," Cal shouted.

Now she felt the same.

The silvery light.

That feeling of nightmarish unreality.

The feeling of being lied to, of being manipulated.

Not to mention whatever it was about that shifter, Clea, that felt so wrong.

The two seers.

Mara not wanting to give them Narissa's name and address.

Mara staring at her, begging her with her eyes—

Alexis refocused on the witch's face.

As soon as she did, everything else faded back.

Alexis watched the features of the woman morph.

They rippled into a liquid smoke, and that was familiar, too... Alexis watched the witch change into another being, right in front of her eyes, her face softening and reforming, as if being melted and shaped in wax. She remembered asking Cal jokingly if Travelers were shapeshifters when they were in bed that first night in Los Angeles.

She also remembered what he'd told her—that it depended on which world they were in, and what level of magical skill they'd attained.

She remembered watching the Red Dragon turn into smoke in the cave in Penang.

His whole face had changed, right before he melted out of the collar that held him.

That collar, which had been the only thing to keep his magic in check.

Only the magical machines didn't work in this world.

They hadn't known it yet, but none of their machines worked here.

"Can you portal us out of here, Lightbringer?" Cal still spoke in a half-shout. "Do you have your magic back?"

Alexis looked down at her arms, at the tattoo bands of Ancients' writing around her biceps and forearms.

She concentrated with all of her might, trying to get them to ignite.

But nothing happened.

She didn't see so much as a pale glow from the tattoos.

She closed her eyes, straining harder, trying to summon whatever she could.

Nothing.

She felt nothing.

It was like a weight held her down, suffocating her light under a mesh shroud.

It felt like the magic in her couldn't take a breath under that weight.

She couldn't *still* be drained, could she?

"No."

Alexis looked at her Traveler mate, and Cal shook his head.

"No," he repeated. "I don't think so. It's got to be something else. A curse. A block on your magic. Some kind of illusion. Maybe even the closed portals—"

His words were cut off by a deafening screech.

It was so loud, it cut Alexis' breath, bringing her hands to her ears.

She closed her eyes, pressing her palms tighter against the

pain, trying to block out the horrible noise, half-afraid it would deafen her permanently—

When, just as suddenly as it started…

It stopped.

It stopped, and the room grew entirely still.

Looking around, Alexis realized it hadn't only been that horrible sound—all of it stopped. The candles had all been blown out. The light, the sound, the ripples of silvery-gold and purple flames… all of it had died.

The glowing of the standing crystal had snuffed out.

Alexis opened her eyes, panting, her hands still clamped over her ears.

The only light left in the room came from the pale, blue light inside the wall fountain, and a blue accent light around the edge of the ceiling.

Alexis had added those little details to the room, too.

She let up on the pressure of her palms when everything went silent. When it remained quiet, she lowered her hands slowly, glancing at Cal, seeing him do the same. Cal's eyes fixed on the table, on the place where the witch had been.

Alexis turned, following his gaze.

The witch was gone.

Alexis expected to see the Red Dragon in her place.

She expected to see Cal's father sitting on that square cushion.

But she didn't.

It wasn't him.

Instead, a different woman sat there. She was around the same size as the witch, but looked absolutely nothing else like the woman who had been sitting there when all of this started. The new woman had a smaller, more elfin face, with short, white, spiky hair, wide violet eyes, a sharp chin, delicate features.

Alexis knew that face.

It wasn't the Red Dragon.

It wasn't Cal's father.

It was his sister, Dharma.

"*T*ut-tut-tut. Don't get excited, brother…"

Dharma smiled, waggling her finger at Cal when he looked ready to rush her.

She darted an equally warning look at Alexis when the Lightbringer reached around for the backpack she still wore, the one filled with weapons they'd brought with them in the hotel.

"Don't even think it, Lightbringer," Dharma warned.

She raised a gun, aiming it pointedly at Alexis' chest.

"…I don't *have* to kill you," Dharma added with a smirk. "But I would very much enjoy it."

Unlike on the Traveler world, Cal's sister held a human gun now, one from this dimension. Which meant it would likely kill her, and kill Cal, if Dharma decided to use it to shoot either of them.

Dharma must have learned the same lesson about how badly the guns and machines from that other world translated for this one.

Shifting the gun's muzzle between them to keep them both back, the female Traveler looked at Alexis, then back at Cal.

She was still smiling.

The smile disturbed Alexis, in part because she realized it was the witch's smile, the same one she'd seen on that very different face, which had worn a much smaller, thinner mouth. The female Traveler rose gracefully from her cross-legged position on the rug, never taking her eyes off Alexis, and it struck Alexis again, that all of Dharma's facial expressions and gestures had also belonged to the witch.

Cal was right.

She'd been right, too.

He'd known who the witch was, without knowing he'd known.

He may have gotten the details wrong, but he'd been spot-on with the basics.

She absolutely stank of the Red Dragon's magic.

Cal's father must have sent Dharma ahead, back on that other world.

He'd tracked them to the Parliament Building on that version of Earth, and he must have worried Cal and his guard might make it through the primary portal before the Red Dragon could stop them. So, Cal's father being who he was, he'd sent his own daughter ahead to *this* dimension, through the open portal gates, likely instructing her to use one of the secondaries on another part of the planet so Alexis wouldn't feel the gate activating.

Knowing Cal's father, he'd done it as a form of insurance.

Knowing Cal's father, he'd done it to make sure he'd win in the end, even if they killed him. He'd still have the last word, even from the grave.

Since he *wasn't* dead, since Cal wasn't as terrible of a person as his father and opted *not* to kill him, the Red Dragon had likely concocted the whole charade they'd been following since they left the hotel.

He'd worked out all the steps needed to bring her and Cal here, to The White Rabbit.

He'd wanted her and Cal to walk right up to his lieutenant of their own volition, and put themselves under his power.

Why? Why such an elaborate ruse?

Certainly there were easier ways to kill them?

Dharma snorted a low laugh, shaking her head.

"You should see your faces right now," she said mockingly.

The female Traveler stepped back from the table, the gun still raised, but now in a somewhat more relaxed manner. She continued to watch the two of them intently, that faint smile ghosting her full mouth. Cal's sister didn't look afraid, or even angry. She didn't look the slightest bit worried that one of them might attack her.

She looked excited.

She looked like a sociopathic child who got to kill something on her birthday.

"Disappointed to see me, brother?" Dharma asked, aiming her gaze at Cal. "I suppose I'm a bit of a letdown, after you'd feared the big, bad Dad boogeyman. From your expressions, I gather you were expecting the old man to pop in here, deal with you himself?"

Cal and Alexis exchanged grim looks.

Alexis felt herself understand, even as she saw the same realization come to Cal's eyes.

"A distraction." Cal spoke it first.

His eyes shifted back to his sister, even as a colder fury whispered off him.

"...Of course," he murmured. "He would want a distraction while he opened the portals himself."

But Dharma laughed at that, as well.

"No, brother," she said, shaking her head at him pityingly. "No. We didn't lie about *all* of it. Just enough to make it clear you're both *complete* idiots."

"What does that mean?" Alexis cut in.

She still held her backpack in front of her body, gripping it in both hands.

She'd halfway fumbled with the top before Dharma raised the gun. She'd managed to unfasten the main clasp and now held it closed with her hand. She didn't dare pull any of her weapons out, not without a distraction of their own.

If she tried it, Alexis strongly suspected she'd get herself shot.

That, or she'd get Cal shot.

Dharma snorted, giving Alexis a sideways look. "You're not wrong there, Lightbringer."

Alexis frowned, but didn't bother to respond.

She tried to think instead.

She needed the gun.

One of her knives, maybe.

She *really* would've liked to have her whip in her hand. She was damned good with that thing. She could sort this relatively quickly if she had her whip.

She really needed that damned whip.

Blinking, she rubbed her face.

Her mind wondered loudly why she felt so tired.

But Cal understood. Cal picked up on it well before she did.

"Gods damn it." Cal gripped her bicep more tightly in his hand. "They drugged you." His fingers tightened more as he glared at his sister. "You drugged her."

His eyes found the top of the stone table, and the tray sitting on top, with its hand-painted china teapot and three cups and saucers.

"Gods damn it," he repeated, his words lower.

Just then, the door to the corridor swung open.

Alexis blinked at the change in lighting.

Someone had turned on the corridor's main lights.

She raised one of her hands to shield her eyes, still gripping the backpack in front of her. She watched as several beings appeared at the door. They walked inside without really acknowledging her or Cal, choosing to bow to Dharma instead, their movements and facial expressions respectful.

Clea, the elephant shifter.

Dahlia, the vamp with the Brooklyn accent from the main floor.

Two more vampires.

Varlan… gods.

Cal surveyed the same set of faces.

His stare swiveled back to his sister. His voice grew deathly cold.

"You're brought us here to kill us then, sister?"

Dharma snorted again. "Kill you? Gods above, brother. Your addiction to drama is positively a sickness."

"Then what? What do you want?"

"He sent me here to get you out of the way."

Turning, she stared coldly at Alexis.

"You, he needs… unfortunately."

Her eyes turned coldly back to her brother.

"You… dear brother… he does not."

With that, she raised a gun, and without preamble, shot him in the chest.

SHADOW AND SOUND

*A*lexis didn't know where she was.

She had been in her club.

She had been in The White Rabbit.

They surrounded her in that private room at the end of a dark corridor.

She'd screamed, seeing Cal crumple to the floor, a bloom of scarlet spreading over the center of his chest. She'd screamed, watching him look at her, watching him try to get up.

She walked over to help him.

She made it most of the way there—

Right before she collapsed.

She lay on the floor, gasping, staring up at the ceiling.

She couldn't move.

She couldn't even close her eyes.

She'd heard Dharma speak reassuringly to all of them, telling them she, Alexis, wouldn't need to be carried totally, that Alexis should be able to walk… more or less… just not entirely under her own power.

Then they hoisted her up to her feet, large hands holding

her up on each side. Alexis' neck lolled, and they put a hood over her head, blinding her.

The same two sets of hands walked her back over the club floor and to the front lobby.

That much, Alexis could discern from the dim sights and sounds all around her, as well as the fact that the club had filled up in the time they'd spent in that back room.

Even under the hood, with her senses dulled, Alexis could still track the direction of her steps, the dim, flickering lights of the corridor back to the main floor, the shadows of the figures moving around her in an obscuring ring.

When they reentered the club's main bar and stage area, the sounds of the overhead speakers and bar surrounded her as well, drowning out everything else. She heard talking and laughter, the clinks of glass and metal, shoes scuffling the tile floor, seductive murmurs, the creak of leather. She smelled sweat and gin, sweeter tangs of mixed drinks and perfume, cologne and the occasional waft of hash or pot.

She even heard the occasional sharp smack, telling her someone likely performed a demonstration on the main stage.

She heard her staff.

She couldn't call out to them for help.

Anyway, Dahlia had been with her kidnappers.

The whole staff of The White Rabbit might be converted to the Red Dragon now.

That, or they might simply be under the vampire's control.

Whatever the truth of it, the strong hands holding her up led her firmly through the main lobby to the front door, and no one tried to stop them.

Then they shoved her in the back of a car.

No one called out, no one asked them what they were doing.

The other guests at the club probably thought it was some kind of sex game.

That, or Dharma and her friends used magics somehow, to get everyone to turn away, or maybe to get them to see something other than what was happening. The Others seemed to be particularly gifted when it came to those kinds of magicks.

Then there was Varlan.

Varlan was a seer.

Cal—

She snuffed out the thought, closing her eyes under the hood.

She couldn't think about Cal yet.

She couldn't.

She couldn't even call to him.

She might only give them reason to shoot him again.

Even so, her mind played it back, over and over.

Dharma raising the gun.

Dharma shooting him in the chest.

What a weird, twisted thing, that the white-haired Traveler shot her own brother, right after telling him they weren't there to kill them both.

"Put another one on her. She can still see too well," Dharma said, snapping the command from the car's front seat. "Gods of the Skies, look at her! She is clearly straining to see out the window. She is trying to discern where she is…"

Alexis *had* been doing that.

She'd been doing exactly that.

Another black hood fell over her head and face.

Dharma had been right about another thing, too; Alexis had thought she couldn't see before, but now she experienced what it felt like to be truly blind. She could see absolutely nothing at all, not even much in the way of dark versus light.

Light and shadow.

She couldn't see the difference.

She couldn't look out the window.

She lost her ability to deduce where they were going after a handful of turns—

"How are you not ASLEEP already?" Dharma complained. "I gave you enough to down a St. Bernard. Or a small horse, for that matter."

Dharma could still read her mind.

Even without Cal there, connecting Alexis to the minds of his twisted, fucked up family, Dharma and her father could still, somehow, read her mind.

"No," another voice said, from the other side of where she sat. "But I can, sister."

Varlan.

Varlan was in the car with them. Varlan, who'd sold them out to the Red Dragon. The master seer Cal warned her about, the one he felt strongly was much more powerful than he pretended.

Alexis slumped against the leather seat, letting her body go limp.

They drove for what felt like a long time.

Alexis could still feel a few things.

She felt the road when it rose under them, and knew it had to be a freeway onramp, based on the sounds. She heard a strange sound of metal under the car's tires, and open space, possibly a bridge. She felt the change in altitudes, and when the road leveled out, she heard the sound of faster-moving traffic. She heard car and truck horns, changes in the sounds when they went under an overpass or emerged from one.

Eventually, the altitude shifted downwards.

They were leaving the freeway.

They had descended back into the city.

She heard the difference when they returned to another narrow street, where all the sounds were closer, and the car began stopping and starting with traffic lights. She could hear voices through the windows again, tuk-tuk drivers shouting, the sound of vendors and crowds and drunks shouting from bars.

They were in a different part of Bangkok now.

Alexis fought not to think about Cal.

She didn't know where Dharma was taking her, but she knew who the Traveler was likely taking her to see.

Cal. She shot Cal.

They'd murdered him.

"Gods above," Dharma muttered from the seat across from her. "You're as melodramatic as my brother." She kicked Alexis' leg, making her flinch, then draw back. "He's not dead, Lightbringer. Father couldn't risk you freaking out... or dying, for that matter... because he'd killed your precious mate. Travelers are like seers. Didn't you know that? My father tried to get to you before you'd bonded with him... but both of you are so far gone now, it's positively nauseating. Varlan took one look at you both, and he could see it. You're well past the point where you could live without one another..."

"She is," a deeper, flatter voice agreed. "They are."

"See?" Dharma said, kicking Alexis again. "It's funny, my father is never wrong. He said you'd go to one of your lame friends, here in Bangkok... that he wouldn't need to hunt you at all. He would just need to get to your friends first. You bought all of it. Mara's new 'mate,' Clea showing up to bring you to your own club. A witch who worked in downtown Bangkok but didn't have a cell phone."

Dharma snorted in derision.

"None of it raised any red flags at all."

Alexis heard the female Traveler smile.

She didn't bother to dispute the brother-killer's claims.

"Gods above. Can't you shut up about that? I told you... I didn't kill him."

Alexis slurred her words, aiming them at Varlan.

"You said... you said she couldn't hear me."

"She cannot."

Alexis shook her head under the hood, biting her lip. "She can."

"No. *I* can. I am sending your thoughts to her."

Alexis frowned. She wanted to argue with the seer, to tell him how stupid that was. If he was somehow connecting their minds, then how the hell was that any different from the Red Dragon and Dharma piggy-backing on the familial connection between them and Cal to reach her? Wasn't it exactly the same damned thing?

Varlan sighed. "No. But I can see how the technical differences might be less important to you... under the circumstances."

"Technical differences?" Alexis slurred. "Gods and sandwiches..."

Dharma snorted a humorless laugh.

"I might have to revise the 'clever' moniker I gave you," she jeered.

Alexis practically heard the Traveler smirk.

"...You really aren't all that clever at all. You never even noticed that Mara was Varlan's captive, not his girlfriend. Varlan here doesn't even *like* females. Do you, cousin seer?"

"Not usually, my princess," the deeper voice said politely. "I am rather more fond of the males of most species. Including my own."

"You see?" Dharma said. "You aren't very observant...

either of you. But then, our Varlan here is a master liar. Aren't you, my sweet?"

"I am a seer, my princess," the seer intoned, his words containing a kind of bow. "I have worked as an infiltrator for centuries. I can only be as I have operated in the world. Out of necessity. Out of expedience."

And you've chosen the side of Darkness, Alexis thought to herself, a little bitterly. *You have chosen to enslave yourself to The Others... to the Red Dragon... a narcissistic fool and blowhard if there ever was one. What a pathetic waste of power...*

She'd always been told most of the old seers were warriors of the Light.

Even the more eccentric ones.

"I have tried what you call 'the side of Light,' sister." Varlan spoke dryly, obviously hearing her mind. "I found I generally fared much better under the beings you call The Others. As I told you before, I have a long history with them. What I might have neglected to tell you is, for most of that history, I worked for them, not against them. We have known one another for a long time… a very long time. While I have not always agreed with their choices in leadership, I must say, they have rarely mistreated me."

His voice grew lower, harder.

"I am unable to say that about the beings of Light. The ones you call the Ancients… the same beings I was raised to call the Ancestors. I was left to fall, through a portal in time and space, and if not for the intervention of The Others, I would have been lost forever."

Alexis didn't try to pull that apart, either.

Instead, she thought over everything Varlan told them at that house in Old Town.

It didn't take her long to realize all of it had been lies.

Well, all the parts of it that mattered now.

"The Red Dragon," she said. "He's not on his way up here by boat. He is already here. He is already in Bangkok."

Dhrama laughed, a delighted sound.

"Moron," she jeered. "You and my brother are *perfect* for one another."

Alexis didn't answer.

When the female Traveler didn't get the reaction she'd clearly hoped for, she leaned back her head, sinking back into the leather seats.

Alexis let her mind fall totally blank.

Thinking now wasn't likely to help her.

"I agree," Varlan told her, patting her thigh in an almost friendly way. "Nothing will help you now. You may as well rest. Save your strength."

Alexis didn't ask for what.

She had a feeling she already knew.

THE PRIMARY GATE

They walked her up a steep flight of stone stairs.

Alexis could see nothing.

It was pitch black under the hood.

She still heard traffic in the distance, but it sounded strangely far away now, like they were in a park of some kind, far away from the main road. Wherever they had brought her, Alexis found herself thinking it was likely a place that closed after dark.

That, or it was simply just deserted.

She felt other beings all around her again, at least ten of them.

She once more grew conscious of not having her weapons.

Or access to any of her magic.

Where the hell was she? Why had they brought her all the way out here? They couldn't possibly know the location of any portals. There were no portals left... none. Alexis had closed them all. Even Alexis could no longer sense anything.

When she stretched out feelers, using the part of herself

that used to know, instinctively, the location of every portal gate in the world...

She felt nothing.

"To open a new one, there must be an appropriate place," Varlan intoned. "It must, of necessity, be a primary portal in the beginning. Therefore, we had to bring you to one of the primary portal locations on this world. It is likely the primary will be moved, after your death... or possibly before... but for now, we needed it out of the way. We needed it in a place we could guard, keep safe from wandering humans and curious supernaturals."

Alexis absorbed his words.

She didn't know the location of all the dormant primary portal locations.

She'd never considered any reason why she might *need* to know the location of a portal that was no longer active. She only went to the primary portal locations when they housed an *actual* primary portal.

But Varlan's words made sense.

It was also the first time Alexis realized the old seer was one of the people holding her up, steering her across the open ground towards... something.

"It is a temple, sister," Varlan said. "And you were correct in your supposition. It is one of the few not open to the public. It is a historical place, one closed for 'renovations.' We can keep it closed for as long as we need. And it is situated in such a way that our people can easily protect it."

Alexis frowned, fighting to hold up her head.

"You would try to install a primary gate here?" she said, her words still slurring over her tongue. "In the middle of a city? Closed or not, it will attract supernaturals from all over... everywhere. There's no possible way to stop them from coming here. Even if you guard it. Even if you push people to stay away… you'll still get people from falling through it on accident."

She shook her head, gasping a little.

"Can't help it," she said. "City of nine million people… supernaturals all over Asia coming here, feeling the gate." She shook her head again. "You can't protect that. No one could. I wouldn't even put a secondary here…"

She swallowed thickly, shaking her head.

"…Vampires. All over Asia. Werewolves. Were-pandas or whatever…"

"It is only a temporary thing, sister," the old seer intoned.

"It's insane," she repeated. "Totally batshit."

"We do not intend to keep the gates open for as long as you might suppose," he replied, clearly unaffected by her words. "We intend for you to open them for our purposes… then to close them again. Your new king, the Red Dragon, has decided to claim this world, your world, first. He will live here, too, at least for now. But he needs more of The Others' influence here. So he will let in his friends when you open the gates. Then you will either close them again yourself, or instruct the Dark Gods to close the gates for you."

"That's… insane," she managed.

Varlan didn't react to her saying it that time, either.

"You will do it," he said only.

"Why in the frickin' *gods* would I do that?" she asked.

"Because we will gut your mate in front of you, if you do not comply," Varlan said. "If you do not comply quickly enough, he is likely to suffer for that, as well. He is likely to have things removed, until you *do* comply, Alexis Poole. Possibly fingers, a hand… or an eye. So I would not suggest you play games in resisting your orders."

Alexis felt a confused tangle of emotions.

"He's… alive?" she said.

"Of course he's alive. We told you, he is alive."

"You lied. About… everything."

"Perhaps," the old seer said, unfazed. "But we did not lie about this. What I told you is true. We could not risk killing him. Not when it might kill you. I was brought in, in part, to assess the mate connection between you."

There was another silence.

Alexis felt queasy.

Partly at everything Varlan had said, partly out of worry they were still lying to her about Cal. She'd seen them *shoot* him.

She'd seen him fall.

At the same time, she *did* know.

She knew he wasn't dead.

She didn't know *how* she knew exactly, but she knew.

Cal was still alive.

"Of course," Varlan said. "He is your mate."

She felt that pain in her chest worsen.

Now they were talking about gutting him in front of her, cutting off parts of his body. Closing her eyes behind the hood, she fought the images out of her mind.

Really, there was nothing she could do with that information.

Not until she saw Cal for yourself.

"That time is coming, my queen," Varlan murmured.

She chose not to try and interpret him calling her that, either.

They dragged her up a last flight of stairs.

She walked somewhat more easily across flatter tile, into a spacious-feeling room where the sounds of their shoes echoed up the walls and ceiling.

Alexis winced at the reverberating sounds, even as she tried to make out how many of them might be in here with her, and whether Cal might be one of them.

Varlan had said it was a temple of some kind.

Unfortunately, so many *wats*, shrines, temples, churches, and other religious markers lay hidden in alleys, neighborhoods, and side-streets all over Bangkok, the information was more or less meaningless.

"Where's Cal?" she asked. "Where is the White Dragon?"

Varlan didn't answer.

Neither did whoever held her arm on the right.

They said they hadn't killed him, but how was that possible?

The thought continued to repeat in her head.

It grew into a near mantra.

"Do not worry yourself with this," Varlan advised. "Worry about how you will summon the beings that will allow you to re-open the doors, Lightbringer."

"But I can't." Alexis shook her head, frowning. "My magic hasn't been working. Not since I closed the portals. I *can't* do it. Why do you think we went to the witch?"

"You will talk to the Red Dragon about that," Varlan said only.

Alexis opened her mouth, about to try again, when the seer jerked her to a stop.

The person on her other side stopped too, and she hung there, between them, and realized they had reached their destination.

She strained to listen, to pick up more information—

—when someone grabbed the hood and ripped it off her head.

THE MANY-HEADED ELEPHANT

*A*lexis found herself standing beneath an enormous statue, inside a high-ceilinged *wat.*

A black-stone creature loomed over her, at least forty feet tall.

It depicted an elephant.

Well… an elephant of sorts.

In this version, the elephant had three heads, each of them in slightly different positions, giving it the appearance of some kind of magical, supernatural mutant of the elephant world. All three of the heads had upraised trunks, long ivory tusks, and open mouths, like they screamed their anger at the human and supernatural worlds.

Alexis assumed it must be some obscure depiction of Ganesha, as she knew of no other elephant god, but she'd never seen a statue or an image of Ganesha quite like it. Something about it struck her as somehow twisted, like someone had taken the likeness of the Hindu god and infused it with Darkness, making it appear threatening, ominous, borderline violent.

Ganesha was usually depicted dancing, his hands articulated in various *mudras,* or Indian prayer positions. He usually looked happy.

Alexis' eyes left the statue, descending slowly to meet the crowd that stood around her.

She saw the Red Dragon first.

He stood there, looking strangely human in a human-style suit, charcoal gray with a white shirt and a deep-black tie. He stood under the same statue, maybe ten feet away, and when someone tore off her hood, she found him watching her warily.

Dharma stood next to him, wearing what looked like Alexis' swords and scabbards on her back. One of Alexis' holsters and Glocks had also been strapped around the female Traveler's waist, opposite the largest of her hunting knives.

Alexis couldn't help but frown, seeing her weapons on the female Traveler, but she didn't let her eyes linger there for long. Still taking inventory, she looked around at the rest of the faces.

Clea, the elephant shifter who'd brought them to The White Rabbit, stood out first.

A handful of vampires Alexis didn't recognize lined the wall behind the tall shifter, along with the vampire, Dahlia, from the club...

And Warrick, who'd been in Cal's security detail.

Alexis' eyes stopped on Warrick.

She couldn't say she was surprised really.

Anger rose in her anyway, tightening her chest.

She may not have ever trusted Warrick, or liked him particularly, or viewed him remotely as a true ally, much less a friend... but Cal had.

Cal had viewed him as loyal.

He may have even viewed Warrick as a friend.

Of course, it was always possible Cal had been more wise to Warrick's true nature than Alexis had realized.

It angered her, anyway.

It angered her whenever *any* being... whatever the hell species Warrick was... would attempt to take advantage of another's generosity or trust, whether they were fully successful in that attempt or not.

"Perhaps he *is* loyal," Varlan suggested from next to her. "Perhaps it is simply that he was not loyal to your mate. Perhaps his loyalties had already been promised to another."

Alexis turned, giving the seer a cold look.

"He is fae, like your friend," Varlan added, nodding towards Warrick. "You wondered about his race. I am surprised she did not tell you."

Alexis frowned.

Her eyes followed Varlan's back to Warrick, and she found herself looking for the hints of fae in the tall male's stature and features. Now that she knew to look for it, she could see it.

He did have aspects in his features that reminded her of fae she had encountered before.

For the same reason, as much as she wanted to doubt Varlan's word, she found herself thinking he was likely telling the truth.

"Well," Varlan amended. "He's not *exactly* like your friend, of course. Warrick is full fae. Not half. He has no human blood in him... not that I'm aware."

Varlan's deep purple eyes turned to hers, still holding nothing, no hint of emotion whatsoever.

"He owed a life debt to the Red Dragon," the seer explained. "Not that it will likely mean much to you, but that can be a strong motivator, when a being owes so much to another. A deep bond lived there. One that existed prior to his assignment to your husband. One your husband was not able to weaken or break."

Alexis didn't answer.

She looked back at Warrick, noting that he wore a human gun at his hip, also from this version of Earth.

Unlike the gun of hers worn by Dharma, Alexis didn't recognize this one.

Then her eyes noticed something on the floor.

Movement pulled her gaze down, even as her throat abruptly tightened.

Cal sprawled there, his chest red and wet with blood.

He was breathing hard, but almost silently, lying on his back.

He looked to be in pain, but also strangely insubstantial. That odd, liquid, smoke-like substance swirled around his limbs, wisping off his fingers and hair. It blurred his features in waves, only for them to crystallize back into sharp angles and lines, reforming his cheekbones, jaw and lips.

He saw her looking at him, and their eyes met, locked.

She couldn't talk to him.

She couldn't even think at him here, but she felt strangely more calm, looking into his violet-colored eyes.

Then Warrick kicked him.

Cal gasped, his back arching as he writhed in pain.

Alexis felt her whole body go still.

She didn't think it consciously, but that kick sealed something in her.

She knew exactly how she would deal with Warrick, if the time came.

"Now, now, Lightbringer," Varlan murmured. "Happy thoughts. You do this thing for your king, and all of this will be over. You will be reunited with your mate. You may even be permitted to reproduce with him... giving your king a grandson. Providing you do as you are told, and operate the gates as he commands."

Alexis didn't bother to tell him how unconvincing she found his words.

Her eyes returned to the Red Dragon.

The older Traveler King had been watching her.

She didn't notice until she stared back at him, noting the satisfaction in his expression.

She raised her voice, addressing the Red Dragon directly.

"Vampires?" she said. "Fallen fae?"

She swiveled her gaze to stare coldly at Warrick, then looked back at the Red Dragon.

"…Now broken, bitter seers, as well? You really do collect the losers of the manifest realms, don't you, Father? You truly are the King of the Dregs."

Her voice grew openly mocking.

"Where are your smoke demons, Dragon? Didn't you threaten me with armies? Telling me they awaited me on my world?"

She looked around pointedly at the twenty or so creatures in the room.

"This is a pretty sad showing, if this is what you meant. I think even the humans wouldn't need to fear you… if this is all you have brought with you as a conquering hero."

The Red Dragon smiled.

Still, she could tell the jab irritated him.

Clearly, he still wanted her to be afraid.

He wanted her to cower.

She'd learned from their last encounter that he was a thin-skinned infant who couldn't stand to hear anything about himself—or anything at all really—but effusive praise or trembling weakness.

She found it strangely reassuring that her impressions of him had been so perfectly accurate.

"It's interesting to me, that you believe yourself to be so special and unique," she added. "We have sad little bullies in this world, too... humans have many. Vampires. Shifters. They are definitely a number of them among the witches. None are very interesting. None are particularly unique. Even the most vile among them is just the same boring personality, recycled over and over, screaming out their impotence and hatred at the world..."

The Red Dragon gave her a cold smile.

"Your attempts to distract me are equally boring," he said.

He descended slowly down the steps to the main floor of the temple.

She found it funny that he planted each foot heavily, clearly trying to make his entrance menacing, like some kind of god descending the mountain top.

"You are pathetic," she told him.

His lips curved in a thin smile.

She could tell he'd heard the thing about the steps, because he began walking more normally.

When she noticed, she burst out in a laugh.

"Wow," she said that time.

He couldn't seem to help himself.

He scowled.

The look in his eyes burned with the hatred of a thousand suns.

Somehow, Alexis only found that funnier.

Shaking her head, she smiled, even as she continued to case the room.

Her eyes glanced past him, noting that he'd been standing halfway up to the altar, which had been re-decorated, likely by the Red Dragon himself. The gorgeous, detailed, Buddhist tapestries had been torn down, and lay crumpled on the stone floor.

Symbols had been painted on the wall behind him instead, in what looked like real blood.

Whatever those symbols meant, they definitely weren't Buddhist, or symbols of any other human religion she knew.

"Well?" she said, swiveling her gaze from the altar to the king. "Are we going to get this party started, or what?"

She whooped out, feeling a strange flood of giddiness as she let go of her normal self-control, her usual single-mindedness.

"Come on, shithead!" She burst out in a laugh, still hanging from Varlan's fingers. "Open the portal! Let's see those Dark God fuckers in the flesh!"

Staring at her, that hatred still burning coldly from his eyes, the Red Dragon smiled.

THE QUESTION SHE ASKED

*L*ike in that room in the back of The White Rabbit… there was no preamble.

No chanting, no cute little chickens or goats sacrificed, no runes or verses solemnly intoned in Latin. No one wore a robe, or held their hands up in a prayer position.

The light simply appeared.

Then it slowly began to grow, those gold and purple flames creating a whirlpool of liquid light in the sky. Strangely, with no ceiling to contain them, they looked significantly more like a portal than they had inside that room in the back of her nightclub.

They all stared up at that light, watching it build.

The vampires stood against the wall, out of the way, and Dharma stood next to their father, gripping the handle of one of Alexis' Glock-17s in one hand. Varlan continued to stand beside Alexis, gripping her arm in iron fingers.

Previously, another vampire had stood on her other side, one Alexis didn't recognize, but he had released her, walking over to the wall to be with the rest of his kin.

Clearly, they thought Varlan could handle Alexis on his own.

Alexis questioned whether that was true.

Right now, while they had Cal, while she didn't have her magic, or any of her weapons, it didn't matter.

She didn't care.

She'd already seen this dance once tonight.

The difference now was, they weren't trying to trick her into speaking to the Dark Gods, not this time.

This time, they wanted her to do it for real… and they were going to hurt her boyfriend (…*Mate,* her mind whispered. *He's your mate, Alexis, just admit it…*) if she didn't do this thing exactly when and how they told her.

"Why the club?" she asked Varlan.

She spoke loudly, nearly shouting again, over the sound of the growing storm as the light rose around the many-headed elephant statue.

"Why didn't you just bring us here to begin with?" she asked.

Varlan shrugged. "The Red Dragon wanted you to come in willingly. He wished to test your abilities before he faced you personally. He was concerned you might be faking your loss of magics. He didn't want to risk losing you if you opened a portal and disappeared—"

"Or just wiped out all of his lame, vampire minions a second time," Alexis muttered.

"Or perhaps that," the seer conceded. "Either way, he wanted to test out what you did inside a more controlled environment."

Alexis thought about that.

Then she snorted.

"What if I'd summoned the Dark Gods?" she said.

Varlan gave her a sideways look. "He would have worked with that."

"He just wanted to blow a hole in the side of my club," she muttered.

Varlan clicked, a sound she barely heard in the rising wind, even with him standing so close.

"That is possible, too," the seer said.

Still thinking about everything he'd said, even as she watched the light grow brighter, more fire-like overhead, she grunted, louder.

"Let me get this straight," she said. "Your new king didn't want to face me until he knew it was safe, so he sent his *daughter* in to face me instead."

"Yes."

She snorted louder. "What an impressive king you've chosen for yourself, Varlan. You must be so very proud."

Varlan shrugged. "Kings come and go. They never last."

"Until they do," Alexis muttered.

Varlan turned, looking at her.

He didn't respond, but for some reason, she got the impression that comment actually got to him.

She stared up, watching the flames begin to swirl overhead.

They looked like a whirlpool now.

Like an upside-down whirlpool in the sky.

Or maybe the simulation of a hurricane, or a typhoon.

"I'm sorry about whatever happened to you on your first world," she said to Varlan, speaking loudly over the wind. "But you're a fucking idiot if you think things are going to turn out better for you, if you align with these things."

There was a silence after she spoke.

For a few seconds, she thought Varlan might answer her.

But he didn't, and then the Red Dragon spoke.

When Alexis looked over, Dharma already stood over her brother, Alexis' hunting knife unsheathed, and gripped tightly in her hand.

"Do it!" the Red Dragon commanded. "I will only ask you once, Lightbringer. Call for them."

So Alexis did.

*S*he didn't know how she knew how to do it.

Really, she didn't *know* how to do it, not in the usual sense.

If someone has asked her how—as several people had, just that day, come to think of it—Alexis would have sworn up and down that she *didn't* know how, that she had no frickin' *clue* how to call for a kind of shady god through a dark vortex created by a psychopathic, recently-deposed Traveler king with ambitions to burn down all of creation.

If Cal hadn't been lying there on the ground, Alexis' own hunting knife pressed to his throat, she might not even have tried.

As it was, she strained herself outwards.

She threw every ounce of her mind, her will, her very essence, towards that vortex of light.

She tried to feel something there.

Anything.

She didn't expect to feel anything.

She expected to fail, and for them to scream at her that she'd done it on purpose.

She was stalling.

She was stalling, hoping something would happen that might change the current configuration of chess pieces on the board.

She strained upward with all of her might, and looked for them, without knowing how she looked, without being able to explain *any* of it to anyone—

Hello?

She hadn't noticed the change.

Suddenly, it was completely still.

Silent.

She stood in an empty space, a gray floor below her feet, gray walls on every side.

She looked around, seeing herself in the same clothes she'd worn down in the wat, while she stood under the three-headed elephant.

Hello? she said in return.

Who are you?

Alexis thought about the question.

She truthfully had no idea how to answer it.

Alexis, she said finally. *I used to be a Lightbringer.*

Confusion swirled around her.

She still couldn't see them.

She looked up at the gray ceiling, but she couldn't see any of them. She felt them though, and for the first time, it really hit her that there was more than one of them.

No one who is a Lightbringer is no longer a Lightbringer, they said.

The voices overlapped, so many of them, she couldn't distinguish any one. There may have been three of them. There may have been three thousand.

She thought about their words.

They felt true.

Yes, she replied. *I see that. Thank you. My magic... the Lightbringer magic. It seems to no longer be working. I thought maybe I wasn't a Lightbringer anymore—*

The voices rose, intoning as one.

No one who is a Lightbringer is no longer a Lightbringer.

She nodded, bowing.

Yes, she repeated. *I see that. I am a Lightbringer. My name is Alexis Poole.*

Why are you here? they asked.

Alexis frowned.

Everything that brought her here swirled through her mind. Running from The Others on Cal's world, the escape of the Red Dragon, the need to re-open the gates before he could plunge the creation into Darkness.

Why are you here? they repeated.

I was sent, she admitted. *Someone sent me. They took my mate. They shot him. Now they are threatening to hurt him more. They sent me here. They want me to ask you to open the portals. They want me to hand over control of the portals to them.*

But you are a Lightbringer.

Yes.

You are a Lightbringer.

Yes, she agreed.

They took... your mate? A single presence asked it that time.

She nodded, feeling a pain in her chest.

Yes. They will hurt him if I don't do as they say.

She felt distress around her.

Anger.

Ripples of confused disgust.

The emotions collided, sliding over the gray surfaces, audible in whispers behind walls of motionless light.

Then, abruptly, the emotions faded.

Again, she could feel nothing.

Alexis looked around. Had she scared them off? Were they angry at her, for helping the Red Dragon corrupt the gates? For risking everything for a mortal being, mate or no? Did they think *her* corrupt, for risking her whole dimension for the son of the Red Dragon?

She was a Lightbringer.

She had been programmed to guard the gates.

According to Dharma, according to everyone, she had been genetically designed to do this one thing... to be trainable, single-minded, deadly.

Single-minded.

Deadly.

She wasn't supposed to care about anything else.

Maybe she shouldn't have told them about Cal.

Had she ruined everything, by telling them about Cal?

I have to help him, she said finally. *Can you you help me? Can you open the gates?*

There was a silence.

If it is wrong, it is wrong, she said. *I would understand. I will honor your decision. But I must ask. He is my mate. I would not ask it otherwise. I would not ask unless it was the right thing for all dimensions.*

Another silence.

You wish help? a voice asked.

Yes! Alexis said. *I wish your help! Help me to save my mate!*

Help for your mate? A lone voice, the same voice.

Is this what you ask us? another asked. *You ask for help?*

The legions of voices rose then, overlapping, strangely happy sounding.

Help, help, help, help... she asks for help... help to save her mate... the Lightbringer's mate, the mate of the Lightbringer, the one who she saves...

She looked around her, bewildered.

Please— she began.

But the voices cut her off.

Will the Red Dragon give you your mate back? If we open the gates?

Alexis found she couldn't lie to them.

She'd always been really bad at lying. Even if she hadn't been bad at lying, even if she'd been the best liar in the world, she couldn't lie to these beings.

I don't know, she admitted. *Probably not. But I have to try.*

Yes, yes... of course. The overlapping voices returned,

echoing around her happily. *You must try. Try, try... he is your mate. You cannot help but try...*

Can you help me? she asked.

The silence deepened.

Then, that single voice rose again, shattering the quiet.

This time, it spoke loudly, vibrating the gray, nowhere space.

Vibrating her whole being.

Making her whole being go still.

YES, the voice said. *THE ANSWER IS YES.*

There was a bright flash.

Then Alexis was falling, tumbling through the sky.

THE ANSWER THEY GAVE

*I*t blinded her.

The bright light blinded her.

For a few seconds, she was lost in a raging storm.

Celestial winds.

The roar of the might of heaven.

A tempest in a teapot.

But only if she was the size of a mouse.

Everything raged around her… blotting out her mind, so loud she couldn't think past it, couldn't breathe, couldn't see…

Then, without warning, it stopped.

Everything stopped.

Alexis was lying on a stone floor.

She sprawled on her back, in a dark room, a high ceiling stretched above her.

Strange, black shadows punctuated her view, creating odd shapes against the high, white ceiling. Open arches let in light from the moon and stars, and the distant, ambient light of a bright city filled with people living their lives.

Alexis didn't move.

She didn't move for what felt like a long time.

Then someone groaned.

A voice she recognized.

"Cal..."

She murmured his name, sitting up in a blind panic.

Scrabbling over the floor, she crawled to him, finding him more by feel than by sight, especially at first. Then she hung over him and she was holding his hand. He gasped, looking up at her, his eyes glowing faintly in the same moonlight that reflected on the floor.

Looking up at her, he smiled, gripping her hand.

"Are you all right?" She fought to breathe, frantic now that she hung over him and couldn't see him. "Is there a light?"

She looked around, still gripping his hand in both of hers, realizing suddenly how quiet it was, how loud her voice sounded.

"Where is everyone?" she muttered. "Did they really just leave us here?"

Cal let out a bewildered half-laugh.

She looked down at him, frowning.

"What happened?" she said.

Cal laughed again, even though it obviously pained him to do it. Wincing, he pressed a hand to his chest, gasping as he fought to control his heaving chest.

"We need to get you to a hospital," she said.

"No." He shook his head. "I know it looks bad. But it's not. I was able to move my matter around. To keep it from hitting anything important... and then to expel the bullet afterwards." Gasping, looking up at her, he shook his head again, gripping her hand. "I'm all right. I promise you, my love. I lost more blood getting out the damned bullet than I did in the original shot. I'm already starting to heal—"

"What the hell happened?" She gripped his hand tighter,

staring down at him in the dark. "Did I do it? Did I open the gates?"

Cal frowned, looking back at her. "You really don't remember? You don't remember any of it?"

Feeling a shiver of misgiving that time, she shook her head.

"Can you feel the gates?" Cal asked next. "Are they open?"

Alexis frowned.

Then she tried to extend her Lightbringer's awareness.

She tried as hard as she could.

In the end, she gave up, gasping a little.

Looking at Cal, she shook her head.

"No," she said. "I still can't feel anything." Thinking, still breathing hard, she pursed her lips. "My magic is still gone. But I think I'd feel them still. I think I'd feel the primary gate, if it had re-opened."

Cal nodded, squeezing her hand in his.

"I agree," he said only.

There was a silence.

For a moment they only sat there together.

Alexis felt so much relief, just having him there, she struggled to think.

"You're really okay?" she said.

"I'm really okay," he assured her.

"What happened?" she said. "The Gods told me they were granting my request. What did they do?"

"What did you ask them for?" Cal said, wrapping his second hand around hers.

Alexis thought for a moment.

Then she felt a sudden shock to her chest.

"I asked for their help."

Cal chuckled. "Well... I'm pretty sure you got that, my love."

Alexis looked down at him, feeling a kind of dawning horror.

"I asked them to save you."

He kissed her fingers, smiling up at her. "I'm pretty sure you got that, too."

"Cal... where is everyone else? Did they leave us here?"

She already knew the answer.

She knew what he was going to say before he said it.

Even so, she couldn't not hear it.

She needed to hear it from him, to have someone tell her it bluntly.

Cal obliged, his voice matter-of-fact.

"A giant, dragon-like, insanely huge thing came out of that vortex of light," the Traveler King said, still squeezing both of her hands. "It opened its mouth, and it sucked every last one of them up. All of them but me. And you..." he added, kissing her fingers again.

"A giant..." she muttered.

"...dragon," he said succinctly. "Yes. It was quite dramatic. I'm not embarrassed to admit I screamed like a tiny child, scared out of my mind. You had already passed out. I feared you dead, to be honest... or soon to be dead. Varlan said your soul had passed through the portal, and I feared the worst..."

Tears came to his eyes.

He kissed her fingers again, pressing them to his cheek.

"Gods."

He let out a strangled kind of laugh.

"Then that... *thing*... came out of the ceiling..." He choked out another strange laugh. "It took my father first. Then Varlan. Then it just... it seemed to suck them all up. Like a wind tunnel... like a funnel cloud, pulling them up into that vortex of flame."

Alexis just sat there, perfectly still.

She looked up at the ceiling, but there was nothing there.

There weren't any scorch marks.

There was no blood.

There was nothing.

Cal gripped her hands tighter.

"Can we go home?" he asked her.

He kissed her fingers, closing his eyes when she caressed his face.

"Gods… Alexis. Can we go home now? I want to go home with you."

She stared at him, confused.

"The gates are still closed," she told him. Her throat closed, and she stroked his face. Tears rose to her eyes. "I'm sorry. I'm so sorry, Cal. I can't take you home. I can't. I may never be able to take you back there—"

"No." He shook his head, gripping her hand tighter. "No. Not that place. Not where I was born. Here. This world. Your home. *Our* home. I want to go there."

Looking down at him, she fought to see him through her blurring eyes.

Slowly, his words penetrated.

Slowly, she realized he meant them.

She wiped her face, smiling at him.

"Yes," she told him. "Yes, my love. We can go home."

There really wasn't anything more to say.

WANT TO READ MORE?
Check out the next book in the series!

LORD OF LIGHT
(Light & Shadow #4)

Link: http://bit.ly/LightShadow04

Alexis managed to stave off the first attack on her world by
The Others, for whom the Red Dragon was just one of many
minions…

…but she still has the problem of The Others, themselves.

Not to mention, the gates are still closed, and something
robbed Alexis of her Lightbringer powers.

With her Traveler mate, her band of friends, a few rogue
angels, and a coven of witches she only half-trusts, she must
find a way to save her world, even if it means allying herself
with beings far darker than any she's ever known.

The fourth and final installment of the Light & Shadow series!

LORD OF LIGHT is Book #4 in LIGHT & SHADOW, a series for fans of urban fantasy, paranormal romance, and supernatural suspense.

OR...
DO YOU WANT TO CHECK OUT A DIFFERENT SERIES BY THIS AUTHOR?

Grab the first book in her urban fantasy and paranormal romance QUENTIN BLACK MYSTERY series!

ONLY 99 CENTS!

BLACK IN WHITE
Quentin Black Mystery #1

Link: http://bit.ly/BlackInWhite

"My name is Black. Quentin Black."

Gifted with an uncanny sense about people, psychologist Miri Fox works as a profiler for the San Francisco police. When her best friend, homicide detective Nick Tanaka, thinks he's finally nailed the serial murderer known as the "Wedding Killer," she agrees to check him out, using her gift to discover the truth.

But the suspect, Quentin Black, isn't anything like Miri expects.

He claims to be hunting the killer too, and the longer Miri talks to him, the more determined she becomes to uncover his secrets.

When he confronts her about the nature of her peculiar "insight," Miri gets pulled into Black's bizarre world, and embroiled in a game of cat and mouse with a deadly killer-- who might just be Black himself.

Worse, she finds herself irresistibly drawn to Black, a complication she doesn't need with a best friend who's a homicide cop and a boyfriend in intelligence.

Can Miriam see a way out or is her future covered in Black?

THE QUENTIN BLACK MYSTERY SERIES encompasses a number of dark, gritty paranormal mystery arcs with science fiction elements, starring brilliant and mysterious Quentin Black and forensic psychologist Miriam Fox. For fans of realistic paranormal mysteries with romantic elements, the series spans continents and dimensions as Black solves crimes, takes on other races and tries to keep his and Miri's true identities secret to keep them both alive.

See below for sample pages!

FREE DOWNLOAD!

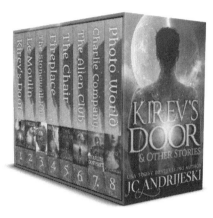

Grab a copy of KIREV'S DOOR, the exciting backstory of the main character from my "Quentin Black" series, when he's still a young slave on "his" version of Earth. Plus seven other stories, many of which you can't get anywhere else!!

★★★★★

This box set is TOTALLY EXCLUSIVE to those who sign up for my VIP mailing list, "The Light Brigade!"

GET MY FREE BOOK!

Or go to: https://www.jcandrijeski.com/mailing-list

REVIEWS ARE AUTHOR HUGS

Hi there!
Now that you've finished reading my book,
PLEASE CONSIDER LEAVING A REVIEW!
A short review is fine and so very appreciated.
Word of mouth is truly essential for any author to succeed!

Leave a Review Here:
https://bit.ly/LightShadow03

SAMPLE PAGES

BLACK IN WHITE
(QUENTIN BLACK MYSTERY #1)

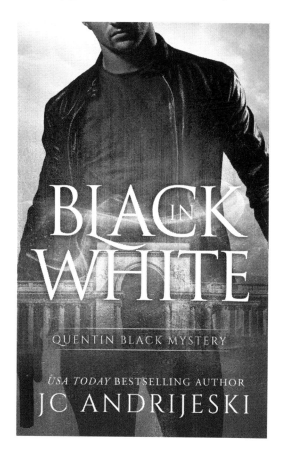

PROLOGUE

PALACE

FIFTEEN-YEAR-OLD Janine Rico was having a good night.

Scratch that.

She was having a *great* night.

An epically awesome night, by pretty much any standard.

First of all, getting alcohol was easy, for a change. She and her pals Hannah and Keeley managed to shoulder-tap some epically challenged, can-I-come-party-with-you-kids loser on their very first try, outside a seedy liquor store on Fillmore. The owner, an older Indian man, didn't care—so loser boy emerged five minutes later with one of the big bottles of peppermint schnapps and another of cheap rum. They ditched him in the park minutes later, running off with two guys from their school and laughing their asses off.

That was like, hours ago now.

The boys had gone home.

They'd been wandering the city most of the night since, determined to make the most of Keeley's mom being out of town and letting them stay in her condo in the Marina District. They'd stopped at a few parks to pass the bottles around and talk and snap pictures with their smart phones, watching the orange-tinted fog billow in odd, smoke-like exhales across the wet grass. They'd already discussed their plans for the next day...which mostly involved sleeping in, along with ordering pizza and movies with Keeley's mom's credit card.

An epic weekend, all in all. Awesomely flawless.

Janine was tired now, though. The cold wind cut her too, even through the down jacket she wore over her hoodie sweatshirt and multicolored knit tights.

It was Keeley's idea to stop at the Palace of Fine Arts before they headed back.

"Nooooo," Janine whined, flopping her arms dramatically. "I'm ready to pass out. I'm cold. I have to pee...this is stupid!"

"Come on," Keeley cajoled. "It's totally cool! Look...it's all lit up!"

"It's lit up every night," Janine grumbled.

Hannah hooked Janine's arm, but sided with Keeley. "We can take pictures...send them to Kristi in Tahoe and make her *crazy* jealous!"

Hannah always wanted to dig at Kristi. Maybe because Kristi's family was rich, or maybe because Hannah was jealous that Kristi and Janine were best friends.

Either way, Janine couldn't fight both of them.

Her eyes shifted to the orange-lit, fifty-foot-tall, Roman-esque columns. They stood on the other side of a man-made lake covered in sleeping ducks and swans, making a disjointed crescent like ancient ruins from an old amphitheater. The fountain in the lake was turned off, so the columns reflected a near-perfect mirror on the glass surface of the water.

As they tromped over slippery grass, Janine found herself thinking it did look pretty cool, with the robe-draped stone ladies resting their arms on top of each column, showing their stone backs to the world. Broken by deep black shadows, the stone faces looked otherworldly. Willow trees hung over the lake, rustling over the water as the wind lifted their pale leaves.

"All right," she mumbled, rolling her eyes to let them know they owed her.

Hannah broke out the last of the peppermint schnapps, handing around the bottle by the neck. Shivering and pulling her down jacket tighter against the wind, Janine took a long drink, choking a bit. The warmth of the burn was welcome.

She thought about school on Monday, and telling the other kids about their night.

Hannah was right. This was *so* going to blow Kristi's mind.

Cheered at the thought, Janine grinned, taking another slug of the schnapps and shuddering when it wanted to come back up her throat.

"I think I'm done," she said, handing the bottle to Keeley and wiping her mouth.

"I soooo want to get married here!" Keeley said, after taking her own drink.

"Me too!" Hannah seconded.

The three of them wandered the asphalt path between orange-lit columns. The path led to the rotunda, but would also spit them out through the row of columns on the other side, and back to the lawn that would eventually let them off at the edge of the Marina District.

Maybe this wasn't such a bad short cut after all.

The columns looked way bigger and taller up close, like something really and truly old. Janine gawked up with her two friends, despite the dozens of times she'd walked here with her parents or during school trips or whatever.

Pulling out her smart phone, she took a few pictures, first just of the columns themselves, then of Keeley and Hannah as they posed, hanging on the base of pillars and stone urn.

"We should send these to Kristi *now!*" Hannah squealed, laughing with her arm slung around Keeley's neck. "She will be *sooo* pissed!"

"No, her mom checks her phone, like, every day," Janine warned. "She would totally bust us if she saw what time we'd sent these."

Hannah's expression sobered.

Before she could answer, they all came to an abrupt stop.

Keeley saw it first.

She smacked Janine, who came to a dead stop, right before Janine grabbed Hannah, gripping her friend's peacoat jacket in a tightly-clenched fist.

Hannah froze.

Before them, a woman wearing a white, flowing dress lay in a strangely elegant pose on the ground. Something about the way her legs and arms were positioned struck Janine as broken-looking, despite the precision...like a store mannequin that had been accidentally knocked over and lay facing the wrong direction.

The woman's legs were almost in a running or leaping pose. Her arms curved up over her head, the wrists and fingers positioned inward like a ballerina's. Her chin and face tilted up, towards the lake, as if to look between her delicately positioned hands.

Whatever caused the position, it didn't look right.

The woman's face didn't look right, either.

It belonged to a porcelain doll. Someone had slathered so much make-up on her cheeks and eyes that they appeared bruised.

Those details, however, Janine remembered only later.

In those few seconds, all she could see was the blood.

The woman's dress from waist to bust-line was soaked a dark red that looked purple in the orange light under the dome. That same splash of red covered her all the way to her thighs, past where the dress bunched up and flared out like the dress of a princess in fairytale.

It was a wedding dress.

The teenagers just stood there, all three of them breathing hard now, like they'd been running. They stared at the woman under the Palace of Fine Arts rotunda as if the sight put them in a trance. Janine found herself unable to look away.

Then she realized they weren't alone.

Next to the woman in white, a man crouched, staring down at her.

Janine must have seen him there.

She must have been staring right at him, along with the woman. Even so, his form seemed to jump out at her all at once.

Her first, irrational thought was: *He must be the groom.*

Then Janine saw his hands reach for the mid-section of the woman on the ground.

He was touching her.

His face remained in shadow. Black hair hung down over his eyes. He straightened in a single, fluid motion and like the woman in white, blood streaked his skin like glistening paint, all the way past his elbows to the edges of his black T-shirt.

His face and neck wore dark and shining splotches of the same.

He turned his head, staring at the three girls.

For the first time, the angles of his face caught the light, displaying high cheekbones and a distinct lack of expression in the sunset-colored flood lamps aimed at the dome. Those almond-shaped eyes looked oddly yellow—almost gold— under that glow of the rotunda.

Janine saw those feral-looking eyes focus on Hannah, then Keeley.

Right before they aimed directly at her.

Her trance finally broke.

A loud, familiar-sounding voice let out a piercing scream. The scream echoed inside the hollow chamber of the dome, replicating there.

It occurred to Janine only later that the scream came from her.

That was *her* screaming, Janine Rico.

In the same instant, a voice rose in her mind.

This one didn't sound like her at all.

Run away, little girl, the voice whispered. *Run away now, little one, all the way home, before the big bad wolf decides to eat you, too...*

Janine didn't have to be told twice.

WANT TO READ MORE?
Continue the rest of the novel here*:*
BLACK IN WHITE
(Quentin Black Mystery #1)

ONLY 99 CENTS!

Link: http://bit.ly/BlackInWhite

BOOKS IN THE LIGHT & SHADOW SERIES
(RECOMMENDED READING ORDER)

LIGHTBRINGER (Book #1)
WHITE DRAGON (Book #2)
DARK GODS (Book #3)
LORD OF LIGHT (Book #4)

BOOKS IN THE ANGELS IN L.A. SERIES
(RECOMMENDED READING ORDER)

I, ANGEL (Book #1)
BAD ANGEL (Book #2)
FURY OF ANGELS (Book #3)
ANGEL ON FIRE (Book #4)
ANGEL WHO FELL (Book #5)

BOOKS IN THE VAMPIRE DETECTIVE MIDNIGHT SERIES
(RECOMMENDED READING ORDER)

VAMPIRE DETECTIVE MIDNIGHT (Book #1)
EYES OF ICE (Book #2)
THE PRESCIENT (Book #3)
FANG & METAL (Book #4)
THE WHITE DEATH (Book #5)

BOOKS IN THE QUENTIN BLACK MYSTERY SERIES

(RECOMMENDED READING ORDER)

BLACK IN WHITE (Book #1)
Kirev's Door (Book #0.5)
BLACK AS NIGHT (Book #2)
Black Christmas (Book #2.5)
BLACK ON BLACK (Book #3)
Black Supper (Book #3.5)
BLACK IS BACK (Book #4)
BLACK AND BLUE (Book #5)
Black Blood (Book #5.5)
BLACK OF MOOD (Book #6)
BLACK TO DUST (Book #7)
IN BLACK WE TRUST (Book #8)
BLACK THE SUN (Book #9)
TO BLACK WITH LOVE (Book #10)
BLACK DREAMS (Book #11)
BLACK OF HEARTS (Book #12)
BLACK HAWAII (Book #13)
BLACK OF WING (Book #14)
BLACK IS MAGIC (Book #15)

BOOKS IN THE BRIDGE & SWORD SERIES
(RECOMMENDED READING ORDER)

New York (Bridge & Sword Prequel Novel #0.5)
ROOK (Bridge & Sword #1)
SHIELD (Bridge & Sword #2)
SWORD (Bridge & Sword #3)
Revik (Bridge & Sword Prequel Novel #0.1)
SHADOW (Bridge & Sword #4)
KNIGHT (Bridge & Sword #5)

WAR (Bridge & Sword #6)
BRIDGE (Bridge & Sword #7)
Trickster (Bridge & Sword Prequel Novel #0.2)
The Defector (Bridge & Sword Prequel Novel #0.3)
PROPHET (Bridge & Sword #8)
A Glint of Light (Bridge & Sword #8.5)
DRAGON (Bridge & Sword #9)
The Guardian (Bridge & Sword #0.4)
SUN (Bridge & Sword #10)

BOOKS IN THE GODS ON EARTH SERIES
(RECOMMENDED READING ORDER)

THOR (Book #1)
LOKI (Book #2)
TYR (Book #3)

BOOKS IN THE ALIEN APOCALYPSE SERIES
(RECOMMENDED READING ORDER)

THE CULLING (Part I)
THE ROYALS (Part II)
THE NEW ORDER (Part III)
THE REBELLION (Part IV)
THE RINGS FIGHTER

JC Andrijeski is a *USA Today* and *Wall Street Journal* best-selling author of urban fantasy, paranormal romance, mysteries, and apocalyptic science fiction, often with a sexy and metaphysical bent.

JC has a background in journalism, history and politics, and has a tendency to traipse around the globe, eat odd foods, and read whatever she can get her hands on. She grew up in the Bay Area of California, but has lived abroad in Europe, Australia and Asia, and from coast to coast in the continental United States.

She currently lives and writes full time in Los Angeles.

For more information, go to: https://jcandrijeski.com

facebook.com/JCAndrijeski
twitter.com/jcandrijeski
instagram.com/jcandrijeski
bookbub.com/authors/jc-andrijeski
amazon.com/JC-Andrijeski/e/B004MFTAP0

Printed in Great Britain
by Amazon